A Bintel Brief

A Bintel Brief

Volume II

Letters to the Jewish Daily Forward 1950-1980

Compiled and Edited by
Isaac Metzker

Translated by Bella S. Metzker and
Diana Shalet Levy,
under the supervision of Isaac Metzker

THE VIKING PRESS   NEW YORK

Copyright © 1981 by Isaac Metzker
All rights reserved
First published in 1981 by The Viking Press
625 Madison Avenue, New York, N.Y. 10022
Published simultaneously in Canada by
Penguin Books Canada Limited

LIBRARY OF CONGRESS CATALOGING IN PUBLICATION DATA
Main entry under title:
A Bintel brief.
Translated by Bella S. Metzker and Diana Shalet Levy,
under the supervision of Isaac Metzker.
Vol. 2 published by: Viking Press.
Contents: v. 1. Sixty years of letters from the
Lower East Side to the Jewish daily Forward—v. 2.
Letters to the Jewish daily Forward, 1950–1980.
1. Jews—New York (N.Y.)—Social life and customs
—Addresses, essays, lectures.   2.   Lower East Side,
New York (N.Y.)—Social life and customs—Addresses,
essays, lectures.   3.   New York (N.Y.)—Ethnic
relations—Addresses, essays, lectures.   I.   Metzker,
Isaac, 1902–   II.   Forward, New York
F128.9.J5M4   974.7'1004924   71-139047
ISBN 0-670-16671-5 (v. 2)   AACR2

Printed in the United States of America
Set in Melior

Contents

Editor's Introduction

The first period of Jewish immigration to America began with Columbus's voyages of discovery to the New World. Ferdinand and Isabella of Spain, the sponsors of the expeditions, were also responsible for the expulsion of thousands of Jews from their country. Louis de Torres, a linguist who served Columbus as a translator and was the first man to set foot on the soil of the newly discovered land, was the first Jewish immigrant. In time, America became a haven for the Sephardic (Spanish and Portuguese) Jews.

The second period of Jewish immigration to America began in 1848. After the Napoleonic Wars and the Revolutions of 1848, an economic crisis in Germany brought about restrictions and sufferings for the German Jews. These difficult times forced many of these Jews to make their way to America. The Sephardic Jewish community, which was quite wealthy and highly regarded, saw to it that the "green" German immigrants were taken care of, even if it didn't care to socialize with them. Before long, most of the newcomers had surpassed the Sephardic elite. Many of them became owners of large stores and other businesses, and also became active in community life.

The stream of Yiddish-speaking Eastern European Jews

that began to arrive in America in the 1880s represented the third period of Jewish immigration. Thousands of Jews who escaped pogroms in tsarist Russia and persecution in neighboring countries flocked to America. This mass immigration frightened some and brought about the passage of strict quota laws, but before they were passed, 2,650,000 Jews from various European countries managed to enter the United States between 1881 and 1925.

When these immigrants arrived in New York, they were herded together on Castle Garden (and, later, on Ellis Island), where they underwent strict physical examinations and answered long questionnaires. Many were detained for minor reasons. For the immigrants who did manage to pass the examinations, new problems would occasionally arise. Not every immigrant had money, or relatives or friends awaiting him, and those without a potential source of income were detained again. The examinations became stricter as the years went by, and immigrants were being sent back by the hundreds. Newspapers published many articles about the terrible conditions on Ellis Island. Among these newspapers was the *Jewish Daily Forward*, the major Yiddish-language daily in America. In 1909 the *Forward* received a letter signed by one hundred Jewish men and boys who were being held on Ellis Island, describing their bitter lot and the dreadful conditions in which they were held.

The protests and articles generated by this letter forced Washington to take notice of the problem. An investigation into the treatment of the immigrants at Ellis Island was begun, and the testimony of the long-suffering witnesses resulted in the firing of the commissioner. A great many immigrants left Ellis Island at long last as free men and women. Their first thoughts were to find work. But most of them had no trade, did not know the English language, and were unaccustomed to the American life-style.

Abraham Cahan, the editor of the *Forward* from its founding in 1897 until shortly before his death in 1951, was eager to help these immigrants. He was aware of their many problems and knew that they had no one to talk to. In 1906 he started an advice column called "A Bintel Brief" (A Bundle of Letters), which was an immediate success. The paper was soon inundated with letters to the editor, which Cahan answered in simple, straightforward language. From the beginning, the letter writers respected him and trusted his advice.

The more intellectual readers of the newspaper ridiculed Cahan, saying that instead of raising the stature of the immigrants, he was stooping to their level in the "Bintel Brief." His answer was that in order to help a child who has fallen, one has first to bend down to lift him up. The poverty of these immigrants was very great, and this was reflected in their letters to the column. This is one of the thousands of letters that Cahan received: "My husband left me and our three children in desperate need. My youngest child is six months old. I want to sell my three beautiful children, not for money, but for a secure home for them where they will have enough food to eat, also warm clothing for the winter and loving care."

The letters from this period, which were collected in the first "Bintel Brief" book, were written by Jewish immigrants who were uprooted from the Old World, and who came to America to build a new life. Their letters can be used as a psychological study of the dreams and strivings of these people. In spite of their difficulties and the hard times they endured, they never lost faith in their new country, and firmly believed that life in America would be better for them and would certainly be better for their children.

As time passed and new generations were born on American soil, the letters changed in ways that are reflected in this second collection, which covers the years 1950 to 1980. The immigrant generation has now scattered throughout the United States, and the writers of these letters find that as they move into the mainstream of society and achieve the much-sought-after goal of "Americanization" they confront an entirely new set of problems—problems that are every bit as baffling and disturbing as those which they encountered as "greenhorns" thirty, forty, and fifty years earlier. The letters

are now about the problems of old age and retirement, changing neighborhoods, assimilation and intermarriage, children
and grandchildren who have moved far away, and about the
wide gulfs separating the elderly, the middle-aged, and the
young. The letters are written by people of all ages—from
American-born men and women in their thirties and forties
(who frequently apologize for their inability to write in Yiddish) to the aging immigrants who are now in their seventies,
eighties, and nineties—and most of them deal with the efforts
made by grandparents, parents, and children to understand
one another's different life-styles, and to overcome whatever
difficulties they have through mutual respect and an aware-
ness of their common group identity and heritage.

Not too long ago, more than 80 percent of the Jewish population in the United States were immigrants. Today, these
Eastern European immigrants, their children, and their grandchildren constitute a community of approximately 6,000,000
people, of whom more than 80 percent are American-born.
The road from Castle Garden to Middle America has not been
an easy one. The immigrant generation and its American children have faced and dealt with many problems—some more
successfully than others—and have gone on to achieve success
in various fields, and to help shape a rich national culture. All
of this is reflected in the "Bintel Brief" letters of the past seventy-five years, but it is a story that is by no means uniquely
Jewish. Many of these letters could have been written by
members of any one of the scores of immigrant groups that
flocked to the "Golden Land" during the late nineteenth and
early twentieth centuries. This second volume of letters, like
the first, is a history of a complex and turbulent time that is of
value not only to students and scholars but to anyone interested in acquiring a new perspective on the ways in which a
"nation of immigrants" has tried to maintain and build upon
one heritage while it struggles to forge a new one.

Isaac Metzker

A Bintel Brief

The Fifties

Worthy Editor:

I turn to you with a serious problem. It's about our daughter, who is twenty-one years old and causes us a great deal of trouble. She is one of those girls who think they understand more than their parents do. She thinks she can act as she pleases, and we have no right to meddle. In most families, such a girl works and earns and pays board to help out in the house. But she doesn't stay on at any job for any length of time, and we have to give her money for everything she needs. This wouldn't matter to us if she behaved properly and obeyed us.

She goes out with her friends, mostly men, almost every night, and she comes home late. When I or my husband say anything, she opens up with a big mouth. She seems to hate us, as if we were her worst enemies, and she insults us even when there are strangers in the house. More than once I've told her we're trying to help her, but it's no use. She won't even hear me out. We have two older children who are already married, but even they have no influence on her, and she won't listen to them either.

We are terribly distressed, because she has surrounded herself with the wrong kind of friends. It's been going on for several years, and it's getting worse instead of better. Now it's not just that she has no respect for us, but we are simply afraid she'll go astray. She says she's twenty-one and can do as she pleases. My husband thinks we should be stricter with her and force her to fend for herself. But I am afraid that if we get too strict with her, she will leave our home.

We don't know what to do, because we can't stand it any more. I see my daughter behaving improperly and I want to help her, but I don't know how. I beg you to advise me.

Thank you,
S. D.

Answer:

When a girl of twenty-one, still dependent on her parents, looks down on them and considers them her enemies, it's not a minor problem. A daughter at that age should feel close to her parents, intimate and friendly with her mother. It is hard for us to judge why it is so different in your case. We don't know any details about it, what kind of environment she grew up in, or how much attention you and your husband paid her when she was young. Therefore we are not entirely certain that the fault lies only with your daughter for behaving in this manner. We have an idea that you may have been neglectful in raising her.

But it is possible that something is bothering your daughter, and that's why she is confused. Whatever has caused it, we would advise you to try to approach your daughter with friendship and kindness. You would achieve nothing with severity. It might also be advisable if you were to go to the Jewish Family Service. They specialize in problems like yours, and they would try to help you.

Worthy Editor:

I read in the "Bintel Brief" about the question whether one should take down from the walls the pictures of one's deceased husband or wife when one marries for the second time. And since this affects so many families, I would like to express my opinion. The *Forward* is my newspaper, therefore I feel free to say something about this question.

Truly, peace and happiness in the home is the most important thing in family life. Husband and wife must strive to attain this, both in the first and in the second marriage. Taking down the pictures of those who have passed away does not erase the shared joys and sorrows of many years. They remain in the memory, and yesterday cannot be separated from today. You cannot shake off all recollections like a duck shakes water from its feathers. This is the most important thing to remember when a man or woman decide to remarry. It must be understood that one cannot forget the past.

When a man and woman decide to marry again, they must agree to be tolerant. To my way of thinking, one should not cast aside the pictures of the departed but do just the opposite. This is the way to start a life together in a second marriage with mutual trust.

I feel that with this approach to the memories of the deceased husband or wife, you can assure the peace and harmony in the second marriage. This is my opinion.

Mrs. H. A.
Texas

Answer:

We gladly print your letter in which you express your opinion on the question as to whether one should remove the pictures of the deceased husband or wife when one remarries in one's later years. It is very important that husband and wife in a second marriage should be as tolerant as possible. And more important, they should be able to compromise, that is, give in to each other and treat each other with understanding.

We agree with you that when two older people marry for the second time they should first realize that they cannot and should not divide the past from the present. They should treat each other with understanding and compromise. If the second party can be generous enough so that he doesn't care about the pictures on the walls, that's fine. But if they disturb the accord in the home, it doesn't matter if the pictures are taken down and placed in an album. Understanding couples who trust each other and wish to establish a harmonious life should, in this case, find a happy medium, a suitable compromise, to avoid any misunderstanding.

Esteemed Editor:

I am writing to you from a small town in Pennsylvania, where I live, and I appeal to you because I know many people read the "Bintel Brief." The problem is that:

We have a synagogue here in our town. Years ago there were thirty-four Jewish families who supported the synagogue and even employed a rabbi. Years went on this way, but every year there are fewer Jews in our town. The old ones go to their eternal rest, and the young ones move out because they want to give their children a Jewish upbringing.

My husband, who was the rabbi, has also gone to his eternal rest and the situation is thus: there are not even ten men left to make a minyan. We don't have a minyan of Jews even for Rosh Hashonah and Yom Kippur. A few years ago we still had a cantor from New York for the High Holy Days, but for the past two years, when we don't even have ten people for a minyan, the synagogue is closed. The six Jewish families who are still left in town go away for the holidays.

The synagogue, which is near my house, facing my windows, stands dark, locked up, and it breaks my heart. So I decided that maybe something can be done about it. Our town is small, but the climate during the summer is very good for people who have hay fever or asthma. Many people come here during the hay fever season.

I thought I would write to the "Bintel Brief," which

reaches so many people, and maybe some couples who are retired and have an income could come here to settle. I want to add that our synagogue has two Torahs and is nicely furnished. Rent is low here, and people who suffer from asthma or hay fever would feel good living here.

I am writing you the name of this town, and if there are any people interested, I ask you to tell them where it is. At any rate, I think that if they came here during the summer, they would find out for themselves. I thank you very much for the opportunity.

Respectfully,
M. G.

Answer:

Though your letter does not belong in this column, we will answer your request and print it. Your description of your town synagogue which has been left empty made a strong impression on us. It's hard to believe that a Jewish congregation in a small American town could suffer such a downfall, because lately many Jewish communities in the suburbs are growing.

We can imagine what sad feelings are assailing you when you look out at the desolate synagogue that stands locked before the windows of your house. It is easy to understand that you would want Jewish people to come to settle in your town and reopen the synagogue. Since we are not acquainted with particulars about the town and don't know how people would be able to settle there, we have no right to convince them to go there to live.

Dear Editor:

I turn to you for advice and I beg you to answer me.

Twelve years ago my wife passed away, and a year after

her death, I remarried. The woman, like me, was about sixty years old when I took her into my home. I was not fortunate in this marriage, but we stayed together.

Now I'm having words with her because, after many years, I've discovered that she has been saving money in a separate account in another city. Her daughter lives there and has been making the deposits for her. I suggested that she bring the money to me, so I could deposit it in my bank in both our names.

But my wife would not listen. She claims that she has saved the money for her grandchildren. I never expected such talk from her. We've lived together for many years, and she saved this money without my knowledge. I can't forgive her for that, and we quarrel about it constantly. It has come close to our separating, but before we do so, I would like to hear your opinion. The money is mine, but she thinks she has earned it. I hope you do not delay your answer too long.

Respectfully,

A Constant Reader

Answer:

We suspect that something must have happened between you and your wife to make her start saving money without telling you. It may be that some action on your part triggered it. But it is also possible that she saved the money because she was influenced by her daughter.

We don't know how much money she has there, but we can see that this has disrupted your family life. If you don't feel guilty of anything, the blame should fall on your wife's daughter. She had no right to meddle in her mother's life to such an extent. She has succeeded in making her mother keep a separate account, but she could cause her mother to lose her husband.

Since we do not know all the details, it's hard to take sides in this case. But we want to tell you that you must both now consider that the closeness and friendship between two elderly people should not depend on the money issue. You must, therefore, try to smooth out the misunderstanding. If you can't do it alone, you must rely on other people whom you both trust, who could help you with a peaceful settlement.

Worthy Editor:

I turn to you about something that has burdened my heart for many years, and now I want to confide in you and ask your advice.

Over thirty years ago I divorced my first husband and soon after married my second husband, whom I loved very much. Then, shortly after our wedding, I found I was carrying a child from my divorced husband. My second husband decided then that we should move to another city, and we did move a month later. I gave birth to a son, and my husband loved him all these years as much, or maybe more, than the other children we had together. My first husband had no idea that I bore his child, and so the years went on. I lived with my dear husband for thirty-seven happy years, and we raised, in addition to my oldest son, three more children, two sons and a daughter, who will soon, with God's help, be married. The three boys are, thank God, happily married.

All his life my husband was an honest worker and earned a good living, but you don't get rich from work. Three years ago he fell sick, and five months later I lost him forever. The little money we had saved was used up on doctors and hospitals, and I was left with a small amount of insurance and my own little house. My dear children help me out, and I am not in need.

Now this is the situation: I recently learned that my first husband is very wealthy. He had also remarried, but divorced his second wife a short time later. He had no children and has been alone all these years. Now the question has arisen—should I let my first husband know that he has a son? And the main problem: should I tell my dear son that he has another father, since I believe he has the right to benefit from his father's wealth?

I don't know what to do because this can be very upsetting. I can't decide for myself how to handle this. I could write a book about my trouble with my first husband in the brief three years we were married, but it would take too much time and space. Therefore I am trying to keep it as short as possible, and I beg you to give me your good advice on how to handle the situation. I thank you in advance.

Respectfully,
Mrs. B. M.

Answer:

The whole story you relate in your letter sounds a bit fantastic. This may be because you didn't give us all the details. Since we know, however, that anything can happen in this world, we concede the facts are as you describe them and that your first husband was the father of your first son.

It is truly not a light matter to carry such a secret for so many years. At first, at least, you shared the secret with your second husband, but now you are the only one who knows about it. We can imagine how difficult it is for you to decide how to handle it. It is as you write that to reveal the secret, to admit that your first son was your first husband's child, is to create an upsetting situation in your family life.

It is clear you have before you a delicate situation. And you must think carefully about how to handle it. Your reasoning that the most important factor is that your son should benefit from his father's wealth and, in a hundred and twenty years, inherit it, is not right. This should not be the reason for revealing the secret to your first husband that he is the father of your son.

Our opinion is that you should tell your first husband and your son the secret. But this should be done carefully and tactfully. You must not place the emphasis on his wealth. It would be good if someone close to you could help you with this. It might be advisable if someone could first talk to your first husband to prepare him, and later you could approach him with proof of the truth. Finally, your son should be told. Yes, it is a very delicate matter which must be handled with tact and understanding.

Worthy Editor:

I appeal to you as a wise, practical man who understands the problems of day-to-day life.

My dear husband and I have been married for thirty years, and we live quite happily. A year ago we married off our oldest son, and our daughter-in-law and our son have made it a habit to have us over every Sunday for dinner. So you'd think everything was fine, couldn't be better! But that is our problem.

When we come to the children on Sunday, the only entertainment is television. We sit down in a dark room and we look at television, both before dinner and after we've eaten. And, as often occurs with young American women, our daughter-in-law is not a great cook. It seems that the dinner is almost always from cans, and we're not used to that kind of food. Especially my husband does not like canned food, so he is not happy when Sunday comes and we have to go to the children. Almost every time before we go, we get into a quarrel.

My husband says it's up to me to tell our daughter-in-law that it's not the proper way to entertain her husband's parents.

When you invite people to dinner, especially your parents, you should not prepare a meal from cans. But I think that I shouldn't tell that to my daughter-in-law, because when you say something like that, you become the wicked mother-in-law. And I don't want to be a bad mother-in-law. I know that I didn't like it when my husband's mother tried to teach me. Our dear daughter-in-law is still young, and in time she'll learn how to treat guests.

My husband thinks it is my duty to talk to her, especially for his sake, since he can't stand the meals she prepares for us. But I know she means well, and there are very few mothers-in-law who can boast that their daughters-in-law want them for dinner every Sunday.

We agreed to turn to you for your opinion on this problem.

Waiting your answer, respectfully,
Z. E.

Answer:

From your letter, it is clear that you have tried to be a good mother-in-law to your son's wife. We do not doubt that you will succeed, because your attitude toward her is a good one.

Yet your husband is not altogether wrong. It would be good if your young daughter-in-law, who has no parents, should from time to time learn from you. It would not do any harm to explain to her that for a Sunday or a holiday she should make a decent meal. She should know, too, that your husband doesn't care for canned food.

We believe that with your kindness and warm acceptance of your daughter-in-law, you should not find it hard to advise her. You can tell her, in a nice way, that it would be a good idea to surprise her father-in-law and make him a good meal he'd enjoy. It might also be good to suggest that she allow you, some Sundays, to prepare dinner in her house. This way she

might learn, little by little, how to make a decent meal. You
realize this should be done tactfully, so that she should not
feel insulted.

Worthy Editor:

Since I have been a reader of the *Forward* for many years,
I hope you will print my letter and give me your advice on my
problem. I could write a great deal about my life because I
have gone through a lot, but that would take up too much
space. I just want to mention here that I had a big family in
America and in the old country too. Now hardly any are left.

My family was among those that the German murderers
annihilated. Only one niece of mine miraculously survived.
She suffered a great deal, but she lived. She is now in Russia,
where she married a few years ago, and has two children.

A while ago I got a letter from my niece telling me that she
was having a hard time. I am an older woman, and not rich,
but I want to help her. I cried my eyes out reading her letter,
because her words awakened in me so many memories of my
former home and my near and dear ones who were killed.

I've already received a second letter from her, and this
time she wrote that it would be nice if I could send her something. She also hinted that she'd like to be with me, because
she is friendless and lonely. The question now is what can I do
to help her? I would do anything to bring her to America. I've
heard that they are now allowing Jews to leave the Iron Cur-
tain countries, so maybe my niece and her family would be
able to come to America. I would undertake anything to help
her come here, but I don't know whom to turn to or how to
accomplish it.

It would be good for me, and for my niece too, if we could
be together. It would be a comfort after the horrible things

that happened to us, as well as to many other Jewish people who lost their families to the Nazis.

Dear Friend Editor, I beg you to answer and give me your advice.

Respectfully,
Mrs. N. A.

Answer:

We can imagine what you lived through when you heard the dreadful news that your family was massacred by the German murderers. That misfortune came to many, many Jews. Who has not had someone close to him lost among those six million Jews who were annihilated? And for you, as for many Jews, it has been difficult to live with the horrible memories. We will not and must not forget what the Germans did, with the help of their allies, to our people.

Certainly the fact that even one member of your family has contacted you must be a comfort, and it is quite natural that you want to help your relative. It would be a good thing if your niece and her family could come to you. But the expectation of her being able to get out of there is not too rosy yet. We must wait and hope.

First of all, you must find a way to help her in the meantime. We feel it would be practical to apply to the United HIAS (Hebrew Immigrant Aid Society); the organization will be able to help you in this matter.

Dear Editor:

We lost a son in the Korean War eight days after he got there. He left a young wife and a little baby. His wife, our daughter-in-law, was always very close to us, and after she was left a young widow, she grew even closer. She is as dear to us as if she were our own child. She has enough to live on and spends most of her time with the baby.

When we became a bit adjusted to our tragedy, we began to suggest to our dear daughter-in-law that she should find another husband, because it is not right for such a young woman to spend the rest of her life alone. She is now only thirty-four years old. But she didn't want to hear of this and answered that until the baby was older, she couldn't even think of it.

In time she made the acquaintance of a young man of her age who liked her very much and proposed marriage. She likes him too, and she introduced him to us. He made a good impression on us, and we think he is a suitable man for her. He earns a good living and seems to be a gentleman. He was never married before, and he loves the baby so much he wants to adopt him, which means the boy would be given his name. The question is: should my dear wife and I agree to this? The man says that it would be easier for the boy at school if he had his name. Our daughter-in-law says she will agree only if we do because, as we said, she is very close to us.

Therefore, we want to hear your opinion. Should the boy be adopted? The man speaks to us constantly about this.

Waiting for your answer,
The Faithful Parents-in-Law

Answer:

It is certainly painful to lose such a young son, and it is difficult to find words of comfort for the parents and young wife who is left with an orphaned child. But life goes on, and you must not grieve forever. Therefore you were right to suggest that your daughter-in-law, the widow, remarry. And you must be pleased that she found a suitable young man who also loves the child.

As to the question of whether the man should adopt the child, we cannot take sides. It is not up to us to advise you on how to deal with such a private family matter. Since you are very close to your daughter-in-law, you should discuss this among yourselves and come to a conclusion.

But we want to remark that this is not an unusual case. It happens quite often that a child is adopted by his stepfather and takes his name. People believe this is quite practical and helps to create a closer bond between the child and his mother's second husband. It leads to better harmony in the family.

But this does not mean that the child should forget his father who is gone. If such an adoption takes place, it is the duty of his mother and stepfather together to see to it that the child always holds dear the memory of his own father.

Dear Editor:

I beg you to print my letter and give me some advice. This is my problem:

My husband and I are, thank God, happily married. We have a son who is already married and gets along quite well. And we have a daughter, too, a girl of twenty-three, and I need advice about her because we don't know how to handle her. Our daughter is very intelligent and attractive, but we parents are worried that she will, God forbid, remain a spinster. She doesn't go out with young men, and I think maybe it's my fault.

The thing is, when she was quite young, in her teens, I warned her not to let boys kiss her. It started when my husband and I once noticed that a young boy, who used to come into our home, kissed her. When the boy left I told her the boy was not for her, that she shouldn't be friends with him, and that she shouldn't let any boys kiss her, because it was not nice.

Our daughter, who was an obedient child, listened to me and promised to obey me. But now she is twenty-three years old and doesn't go out with young men. This made me think that it's my fault that she has no dates. I think it may be because I told her she shouldn't let boys kiss her. She never had many dates with fellows, but now we're worried because she doesn't look for friendships with men.

Now the question is, should we talk to our daughter and explain that a kiss from a man is not a terrible thing? We are afraid she will think we're giving her permission to be more free than she should.

Dear Editor, give us an idea what to do. I am very worried and simply can't sleep nights. I turn to you because you once helped me with your advice, so I hope you can help me now with a good suggestion. Shall I talk to her or leave it to time?

Respectfully,

T. S.

Answer:

We do not believe you have enough grounds to blame yourself for the fact that your daughter does not go out with young men. Teaching your little daughter how to behave when she was growing out of her baby shoes, and telling her not to kiss the boys she met, was quite natural. Most parents who are concerned with their children and try to protect them from harm act the same way.

In general, we do not believe that your telling your young daughter not to kiss her boyfriends has anything to do with it. The fact that she now goes out seldom and is not anxious for male companionship has more to do with her nature. It may be that she has had a disappointing relationship that you know nothing about.

Whatever the reason, you should not make a tragedy of it and be so upset over the fact that your daughter, at the age of twenty-three, is not yet married. She is still far from being a spinster, and you should not be so worried.

Dear Editor:

Since I often read in your fine "Bintel Brief" your good advice to everyone who appeals to you, I come to you, too, to ask your counsel.

I am writing to you about a brother of mine who passed away a few months ago, at the age of fifty-eight. He was an author who wrote in English, and his wife, a gentile, was also a writer, and they had a happy life together. They had no children. While he was alive, my brother said he wished to be cremated when he died. And his wife carried out his wishes: she had a Jewish funeral service conducted, then she had the body cremated. She took the ashes as a remembrance and kept them for a while in an urn in her house, but this worked on her nerves, and the doctor told her to have the ashes removed from the house. She then had the urn placed in a vault where they keep ashes of other people who were cremated. The woman said that if she might someday move away from the city where she now lives, she would always take the ashes along. She loved him very much, and he loved her too.

But I, as her husband's sister, am brokenhearted over this, and I would like to ask her to send my brother's ashes to me. I would like to have the ashes buried in the cemetery where our parents and another brother are buried. It would be a remembrance for me. And I would be content if my brother's ashes were buried at the same cemetery with my near and dear relations.

Dear Editor, I would like your advice. I beg you, answer me soon. Should I ask her to send me the ashes or not? I will take your advice, and whatever you tell me, I will do. I ask you to answer me as soon as possible, and I thank you very much.

Respectfully,
The Grieving Sister, R. T.

Answer:

As a sister of the deceased, you could approach your gentile sister-in-law with the request that she send you her hus-

band's ashes. But the matter is not as simple as you imagine.

First, there is a question as to whether your brother wanted his ashes to be interred in the cemetery where his parents lie. And then there is also a question as to how his widow will answer you.

It is possible you will get your sister-in-law to agree to your request. But then you must evaluate whether it is right to bury the ashes near your parents. Possibly it would not be fitting to the spirit of your parents. Finally, there is a question as to whether you would be allowed by the congregation or the benevolent society to bury ashes at their cemetery.

Therefore we feel you should consider all these issues and, if everything is in order, then go to your brother's gentile widow with your request.

Dear Friend Editor:

I turn to you for advice as a constant *Forward* reader, and I hope you will be able to help me.

I have been married to my wife for thirty-six years, and we have two children—a son and a daughter who have been married a long time and are independent. I make a good living, and everything would be fine if I didn't have this problem. We have a car, and my wife only wants to teach me how to drive. I have been driving over twenty-five years in my business, but recently I bought a new car for my wife and myself so that we might drive out together. Because of this car, however, my troubles began.

When I drive out to visit the children with my wife, I become so nervous and tired, I feel as though I did a hard day's work. This is because my wife is a back-seat driver. She sits next to me and gives orders. I constantly hear, "Look where you're going." "Drive to the right." "Go left." More than once she grabs my hand while I'm driving, and it scares me to death. She sometimes becomes hysterical and begins to yell when she thinks I'm too close to another car. In short, it has gone so far that I feel like giving up the car.

A week ago, when we were both driving to our daughter's house, she got me so upset that I left her sitting in the car at a gas station and took a taxi to our daughter's. And don't ask what went on when she got to our daughter's house by taxi! From that time on I have trouble every day. I tell her that if she wants to go somewhere, she should go by taxi. And most of all I am upset because our daughter says she is right, although our daughter drives a car herself, and when her mother is with her and starts giving her orders about driving, she says, "Keep quiet, Mom." But if I try to say something, I'm an ogre and worse!

I ask you, please tell us who is right, because I'm afraid it may reach a point where I'll have to leave home. I ask you to answer me as soon as possible and give me your advice.

With respect,
S. T.

Answer:

From your letter it is clear that one never knows where or what can bring trouble to a person. You wanted to bring pleasure into your lives by buying a car, and instead you created trouble for yourself.

Nevertheless, you shouldn't talk about leaving home. Since before you bought the car you always got along well with your wife, there is no reason why there should not be peace in your home now. You know your troubles started because of the car, so you have a solution—give up the car! You got along all these years without a car, so you can get along without it now, unless your wife will agree once and for all to stop being a back-seat driver. The question is: will she be able to control herself and stop telling you how to drive?

If your wife is against your giving up the car, she must

realize that two people cannot drive a car. The cars are built
so that only one person can be at the wheel. She must be
made aware that such back-seat driving can be dangerous
and might lead to an accident.

You have to make certain that your wife understands this.
She has to agree to one or the other—either she agrees to give
up the car, or she has to agree to keep quiet when she rides
with you.

Worthy Friend Editor:

I turn to you for advice and your opinion, as a long-time
reader of the *Forward,* and hope you will print my letter.

I have been married to my dear husband for forty-two
years, and we have four children, may they be healthy, who
are also, thank God, all married. We have a great deal of pleasure from the three older children, but our youngest daughter
causes us a great deal of worry. She got married at the age of
eighteen to a boy she knew only a few weeks. It was during
wartime, and she married him when he was in the army.

Right after the wedding he was shipped overseas. A few
months later she got the telegram with the black border, telling her he was killed. Naturally, she was brokenhearted. As a
widow she received ten thousand dollars from the government. Two years later she married a gentile man who was over
twenty years older than she.

You can well imagine how this affected us, because we are
well-respected in this town. She did not confide in us, and we
could not stop her from doing such a thing. They were married, and he took her away to another city where he owned a
restaurant.

She lived with him for twelve years, and they had no children. Last year he died from a heart attack and left her a great
deal of money. We found out about it from strangers, because

during all those years we did not correspond, and she haɑ come to see us only twice. Now we received a letter from her telling us she would soon marry a Jewish man, about whom we happen to have heard because he is a fine, upstanding person. I don't know if this is permissible under Jewish law, but she writes they will be married by a rabbi, and she asks us to attend the wedding.

My husband says he will not go because he feels ashamed and wants no more to do with her. I think, though, that we should go. Therefore, I appeal to you for your advice, and we beg you to answer soon.

With heartfelt thanks,
A Mother

Answer:
There is no lack of such tragedies, and there are many such troubled parents. But when it happens that the daughter gives up or loses her non-Jewish husband and wants to return to her roots and her family, her parents are usually the first to welcome her with open arms.

We say this in reference to your daughter. If she now marries a Jewish man that you, yourself, say is a fine and decent person, and if she wants you near her when she goes to the altar, you must not refuse to go. She is, after all, your own flesh and blood, and if you can draw her back into your family circle you must not miss the opportunity.

We feel that your husband should listen to you and must not be so stubborn. Usually parents can forgive and forget.

Dear Mr. Editor:
Please excuse my writing to you in English. Although 1 know Yiddish it is a lot easier for me to express myself in

English. I am writing to you because I know that the *Forward* does a lot to help its readers, and I hope that you will be good enough to print my letter in the "Bintel Brief" column that is read by many thousands of people. Maybe there will be someone who can give me the necessary information. The story is this:

I am a man of thirty-six and already have a family. A short time ago I found out that I was adopted by the parents who raised me, and I will have no peace until I find out who and where my real parents are. In all my questioning and searching I have been able to get a few facts, which I will give you in the hope that one of the thousands of *Forward* readers who read my letter will have more information about my real parents.

I was born out of wedlock in St. Marks Hospital in New York on July 24, 1923. My mother was born in Europe and came to America when she was very young. She worked in a New York department store, where she met my father. After I was born they gave me up for adoption. These are all the facts I could discover.

I beg anyone who has any more information about this to write to the "Bintel Brief" column of the *Forward* without using my name, because I don't want to cause any pain to the parents who raised me and gave so much love and devotion to me and my family through the years.

Hoping you will grant my request to print my letter, I thank you very much.

With respect,
A Reader

Answer:

We gladly print this letter and hope that the writer will find his real parents and thereby bring joy to a deserving person. To our best knowledge, we have had a number of similar letters printed in the Forward, and in several instances the people sought were found, which was a happy event in their lives.

Dear Mr. Editor:

In 1939 I brought my father, mother, and brother over here from Europe. My father is now gone; my dear mother, may she live and be well, is ninety-six years old and feels well. She lives with my brother and his wife, who have no children and who both work. But I do not get along with my brother's wife, and she doesn't permit me to come see my dear mother except on Saturdays or Sundays, when they are both at home.

However, I live twenty miles away from them, and I would like to visit my mother when it is more convenient for me, and oftener. But it is hard to get along with my sister-in-law. I would like to add here that my brother and I were the only ones left alive of our parents' six children; the others were killed by the Germans. So I am the oldest now. You understand, I don't want to start a quarrel, therefore I turn to you for a suggestion. How can I arrange to see my mother oftener? Hoping to hear from you as soon as possible, I thank you in advance.

M. V.

Answer:

We don't know what occurred between you and your sister-in-law, and it is not clear to us why she doesn't want you to come to see your mother when you have time and it's convenient. It could be that she has her reasons for her attitude toward you, but whatever the reasons are, we cannot justify her actions.

Your sister-in-law should realize that it is not right to deprive an old woman in her declining years of her little plea-

sure in visiting with her son. Nor do we understand why your brother permits this.

Since we do not know the particulars, nor what your brother and his wife have to say, it is difficult for us to intervene in this case. Therefore we feel it would be advisable to talk this over with someone in the family, or a close friend of the family, who would know what's going on among you.

Possibly, with the intervention of a family member or a friend, you could come to a better relationship with your sister-in-law. Maybe she has some complaints against you that could be straightened out. If it's something she feels you've done wrong, you could give in to her, even if you feel you're not guilty. Everything must be done to settle any misunderstandings as soon as possible, so that you could see your elderly mother more often.

Dear Editor:

I have been a reader of the *Forward* for many years and want to write to you about my sad life and unburden my heart.

I was born of poor parents, one of four children. I had to go to work when I was quite young in order to help provide food for the family. At work, I met a boy of seventeen—I was then fifteen. I went out with him for two years and fell deeply in love. But he came from a wealthy family, and his mother demanded several hundred rubles as dowry, which we didn't have. Meanwhile, we saw each other every day in secret, and I believed he loved me as much as I did him. Mine was a false hope, but I lived in my beautiful fool's paradise till once we lost our self-control, and to my misfortune and shame to my parents, I became pregnant.

At first he comforted me and promised to marry me soon, but when he told his mother about it, she immediately packed him off to America, and he left me without a good-bye.

I was left shamed and shattered and alone at home with my heartbroken parents. They were ashamed to face people, and I stayed in the house all of the time and bewailed my misfortune. When my time came, I gave birth to a beautiful, healthy girl. My mother, in her despair, sent me to a village where I left the child with a peasant woman. I had no other choice. And a few months later, an uncle of mine brought me to America. I hoped to find my boyfriend here, but to my great sorrow, I could not locate him.

Time passed quickly. I met a fine young man and soon married him. Our marriage was happy; he did everything for me, earned a good living, showed me love and tenderness—but I never told him the secret that always lay heavy on my heart. We had three sons and a daughter, all fine, successful children. We lived together for forty-three happy years, and married off all our children. And the second great tragedy in my life came when death separated us.

The terrible loss shattered me physically and spiritually. I had to give up my beautiful home, and because of my health, I find myself here in a convalescent home, where I have enough time during the sleepless nights to relive my whole tragic past. No matter how I try to stifle this in myself, I remember that somewhere in the world I have a daughter who would now be forty-five years old. She is never out of my mind, and I have never found any consolation. Lately a thought has come to me—who knows, maybe her father, my one-time lover whom I've long forgiven for his injustice to me, is somewhere in America. And maybe there are countrymen here who remember this sad life story. I beg them to get in touch with me through the *Forward*.

I thank you and wait for an answer.

A Woman from Kiev

Answer:
Your letter, in which you reveal your secret that you never disclosed to anyone, has moved us deeply. We can imagine

how heavily the secret weighed on your soul and what a sorrow has torn at your heart all these years.

We accede to your request and print your letter in which you describe the misfortune that befell you in your youth. But it is questionable whether anyone would know about the tragedy that occurred so many years ago. We do not want to dishearten you however, and we want to hope, along with you, that someone will reply to your letter.

Dear Editor:

I turn to you for advice about our young daughter, who has a serious problem.

Our daughter was married only ten months ago, when she was not quite eighteen, and her boyfriend was only a year older. We were very opposed to the match, first, because they were both too young—they are childish and don't understand the responsibility of marriage. And second, because the boy seemed to us to be a very stubborn person. He is one of those young men who think too much of themselves. And in addition to all this, his earnings as an office boy are not great.

We couldn't talk our daughter out of this marriage, no matter how we tried. They were married quietly by a rabbi and told us about it only afterward. Since they were already married, we wanted to forget our misgivings, and we accepted him as our child. We helped them furnish three small rooms, and our daughter also went to work—so they lacked for nothing.

It turns out, however, that they are both very childish and don't understand the problems of life. Five months later she became pregnant, and the last time they visited us, he said that when the child was born, they would give it to his mother to raise because our daughter would have to go back to work.

He figured out that this was the only way they could manage, because with a child at home, his wife wouldn't be able to go to work. But our daughter doesn't want to hear of this because his mother lives in another city. They have been quarreling about this, and he has warned our daughter that if she doesn't agree, he will leave her. But she is just as stubborn as he, and they have frequent arguments about this although they love each other. I don't know how to help them because we are not wealthy, and in addition, my husband is not well and I won't be able to help her with the child in any way.

I ask you to give me some advice. What shall I do so they don't break up their home?

With respect and thanks,
Mrs. A. A.

Answer:

It would certainly have been better if your daughter hadn't married so soon. If she and her husband were more practical, they would have realized that they couldn't afford to have a child so soon. It is done, however, and it makes no sense to talk about it now.

The question is: how should the young couple arrange things when the child is born? The plan that your son-in-law came up with is absolutely worthless, and it is natural that your daughter won't accept it. A young, healthy mother doesn't give away her first child. There are plenty of poor families with young children, but they keep them at home. They would go on welfare rather than give up their children.

We are almost certain that your son-in-law will soon see that his plan is not a good one. And he will see it when the child is born and is close to him. Then he, just as the mother, will not want to give him up.

If there are no possibilities that your son-in-law will begin to earn more on his present job, then it might be practical for him and your daughter to move to the city where his parents live. Perhaps it will be easier for them to get settled there, where his parents can give them some help.

Dear Editor:

I am a young woman, and I turn to you for advice. I hope you can help me, since I have no one to turn to and my dear aunt urged me to write to you.

I have been married for four years to a fine man, but he demands that I act and do everything like his mother does. I have nothing against my mother-in-law, but I have other ideas and a different outlook on life. But he wants me to copy his mother in every way, even to rear our three-year-old son as she says. When I start to answer him, to show him that a wife should have more to say than a mother, he makes fun of me. He says a man's true family are his father and mother; a wife is only a wife, like a business partner or a girlfriend, and I can't prove to him that he's wrong.

I have not made a fuss over it all this time. I thought that he'd come to realize he was wrong and would not let his mother rule him, but as time goes on the situation gets worse. Most of all, it saddens me that his mother treats him as a little boy or a mentally retarded person, and he not only doesn't mind it, he doesn't even notice how mean she is to him. I can't discuss it with my mother-in-law because she won't let me talk to her. It wouldn't help anyway, because she is totally wrapped up in her self-esteem.

I can't stand my husband's treatment any more, and I don't want to be second to his mother. I ask you to give me your advice on how to handle this problem, and I will thank you from the bottom of my heart.

With anticipation and respect,
Mrs. R. K. B.

Answer:

It seems that you yourself are much to blame if you are playing second fiddle with your husband and the chief ruler is

*still his mother. Immediately after your marriage you should
have shown your strength. You should not have let it slide.*

Certainly a son or a daughter should be close to parents
after marriage. Certainly your husband has the right to see his
mother often. But that doesn't mean he should let his mother
run him or dictate to you how to run your home life.

The fact that you didn't make a fuss during the early
years was wrong. You should have immediately told him in
no uncertain terms that you would not stand for it. You
should have influenced him to see, once and for all, that it
made no sense to cling to his mother's apron strings and run
to her about every trifle.

But it is not too late to make the change now. Your husband must be made to realize how unhappy you are over his
actions, and the sooner he sees that it cannot go on this way,
the better it will be for you and for him, too.

The Sixties

Dear Friend Editor:

I am writing you this letter and tears are streaming from my eyes. I am so distressed and I need your wise advice.

I am a brokenhearted mother, a widow, and it cost me and my husband, of blessed memory, a lot of effort to raise our three children—a daughter and two sons. Our daughter has been married for many years and has grown children, blessed be the Lord. My youngest son is to be married soon to a girl he has been going with for a long time. My middle son lives with me. This son was wounded in the last war, and only medical miracles saved his life. Both his legs are crippled, and he cannot walk without crutches. He is a fine and gentle person, and I hope to God that he too will find his true love. And now for my problem:

My son and his girl set the date of their wedding two weeks ago, and they asked my wounded son to be best man. It seems that the bride-to-be discussed this with her mother and now regrets that she agreed to have my wounded son as best man. She says that since she did agree, she feels she shouldn't change her mind now.

I ask you to answer me immediately and give me your

advice. How should I handle this? We are all very upset and your advice will, I'm sure, do us all a lot of good.

I thank you in advance.

With respect,
Mrs. S. F.

Answer:

Who the best man at the wedding should be is not important. This should be left to the bride and groom to decide. We think they chose correctly when they asked your wounded son to be best man. This veteran who faced the enemy bravely surely deserves this honor and show of love.

If your son and his bride made a decision, it should stand. The bride should have no regrets. And if the bride's mother is at fault, she should be severely censured. She should never have interfered. Both she and her daughter should realize that it is not an embarrassment to have a wounded veteran act as best man.

Our opinion is that it should be as your son and his bride originally decided. However, if the bride is really against it, it doesn't pay to make an issue of it. There is no sense in quarreling about such things.

We want to take this opportunity to tell your son's future mother-in-law that for her own good she should refrain from giving her daughter advice as to how to act and what to do. She should realize that her interference could upset the peaceful relationship of the young couple.

Dear Editor:

My husband and I have been married over thirty years and some time ago we married off our children, from whom we have great pleasure. But at one time we had a great deal of worry over our eldest daughter.

Our eldest daughter is married to a fine man who is well off. She has a beautiful home, and her husband caters to her every whim. But the old saying that "nobody has everything" is true—our daughter cannot have any children. She went to various doctors, but they couldn't help her. She and her husband were very upset about this, and finally, after six years of marriage, they adopted a little girl who was just a few months old, and my daughter, since then, has been a different person.

The child is being brought up by my daughter and son-in-law as if she were their own, and they love her very much. The little girl, now over five years of age, is clever and as beautiful as an angel.

But lately the question has arisen between my daughter and her husband as to whether they should, in time, tell the child that they adopted her. My husband and I told them that it would be good to tell the child the truth little by little, so that she would understand it as she grew older. But my daughter and son-in-law do not want to hear our opinion. They think that the child need never find out that she was born to other parents.

We often discuss this with our daughter and son-in-law, and we tell them the best way is to tell the truth. We know of other cases where adoptive parents told their children who they are, and the children did not love them any less. But our daughter and son-in-law don't want to hear of it.

Therefore, we would like to hear your opinion on this question, and I write you this letter and beg you to answer soon.

Awaiting your answer, I thank you in advance.

Respectfully,
Mrs. G. G.

Answer:
It is difficult to intervene in such a family problem and tell the parents how to handle their adopted child. But we want to tell you that we agree with you and your husband. We also feel that it is quite practical to tell the child the truth, little by

*little, as she is growing up. One can never know how the truth
might come out unexpectedly. Someone else could inadver-
tently blurt out the story to the child, and it could have a bad
effect.*

*You certainly had the right to express your opinion to
your daughter and son-in-law regarding this situation. But
now you must not be too insistent that they act as you wish.
The child is theirs, and they must decide for themselves.*

*Leave it to time. Perhaps in a few years they will realize
that they must tell their adopted daughter the whole truth. In
any case, there must be no quarrel with your daughter and
son-in-law over this question.*

Dear Editor:

I write you this letter about my niece, daughter of my
sister, who has a problem. This is the thing: when my niece
was a child of eight, her father divorced my sister for another
woman. He has not remarried to this day. My sister didn't
remarry either and always considered this man who shamed
her so as an enemy. But he used to see the child quite often.

He always gave his daughter lovely presents, and she
loved him very much. And he gave my sister a check every
week for the child's support. Even now he sends in a check
every week, though my niece has been working in an office the
past three years and earns a good salary. My sister, too, was
well off.

My niece is going out with a fine young man, and they will
soon be married. Her father told her he'd provide the money
for a beautiful wedding. These days this will amount to several thousand dollars.

My niece is quite pleased with this, but my sister says that
if he comes to the wedding, she will leave. She doesn't want to
see his face after he shamed her so. She doesn't even want him
to assume the expenses of the wedding.

I can't begin to tell you how upset and confused we all are. My niece has begged her mother and cried, asking her not to be so stubborn. And I tried to talk to her, but she wouldn't hear me out. We don't know what to do, or how to act. And my niece is very anxious to hear your opinion about this. My sister is always impressed with your wise advice, and we hope that perhaps your words will have a good effect on her. I beg you to answer soon, and I thank you in advance.

Respectfully,
Mrs. A. K.

Answer:

Though we are not familiar with the details of the break between your sister and her husband, we can understand the present problem. In these circumstances, no matter what plans are made for the wedding, it will not be what you expect. These are, after all, the aftershock waves from that original separation that upset your sister's life so many years ago, and very little can be done about that.

It is not up to us to judge who was guilty in the original breakup, but now there is no other way than for your sister to give in to her daughter. We can imagine how difficult it is for her to face her former husband, especially at her daughter's wedding. He must have hurt her enough, and the encounter will surely bring back memories she doesn't want to recall. But there's no other way than for her to yield and give in. She cannot and must not deprive her daughter of having her father at her wedding.

There is also a question as to whether they should plan such an elaborate wedding. The bride's father should understand that no matter how expensive and how lovely everything will be arranged, the happy occasion will still be overshadowed by a tense feeling. But no matter how the wedding is arranged, your sister must take into consideration the feelings of her daughter, because this is the most important day of her life.

Worthy Editor:

Recently I read that there are mothers who hate their children, so I hope you will allow me to give you my opinion about it.

I know a woman, still quite young, who gave birth to her first child and never gave her any love, though she was a dear little girl. The woman wanted nothing to do with the child, and the grandmother had to take care of her. This went on till the child was three, and then the young couple, that is, the child's parents, were divorced. The man took the child with him, and he's now very happy with his second wife, because she loves his child. The little girl doesn't even know that the woman she calls "Mama" is not her real mother.

The child's real mother has not yet remarried. She doesn't miss her child, who is now eleven, a pretty, clever girl. I don't know what to call a woman like this, except to say she is not in her right mind. I see her sometimes, going around the streets all dressed up as if she were completely free of care. I know there are mothers who get angry, even bad mothers, but it's the first time I've ever seen a mother who doesn't even want to know about the child she bore. I wouldn't believe there was such a mother in the world if I didn't know her.

I would like to hear your opinion of this kind of woman.

Respectfully,
Mrs. D. N.

Answer:

Yes, anything can happen in this world, and it does happen that a mother takes a dislike to her own child. But we cannot say that it is natural for a mother to hate her child, her own flesh and blood. It happens, but it is not natural. It could happen if the mother is not normal, and sometimes it's a case for a psychiatrist to probe the deep-seated reasons that lead to a mother's casting off her own child.

It is known that not only with humans, but also with animals, birds, and fowl, that mother-love is very great. But even with dumb animals, there are exceptions. A duck is ready to spit in your eye if you dare to touch its duckling. The same holds true for a goose. A mother bird begrudges herself a worm or a seed as long as she hasn't fed her nestlings. And the fluttering and chirping of the mother bird is heartrending when she comes to her nest and finds the fledglings gone. The anxiety and sadness of the cow whose suckling calf is taken to the butcher is indescribable. She doesn't stop mooing, day and night. She doesn't want to eat, she loses weight, and for days she doesn't give milk.

But there are irresponsible creatures, such as the cuckoo, who do not care about their offspring. The female places her eggs in strange nests and wants nothing to do with her children. And this happens sometimes with human beings, too.

Worthy Editor:

My husband and I belong to a benevolent society, and a few years ago a group of women from the society formed a Ladies Club. We meet once a month, each time at another woman's house, and we pass the time pleasantly together. It's not a large group of women, but in addition to serving refreshments when we gather, we do a little social service work, too. We raise some money for various philanthropic causes, especially for Israel.

We stay together, and we enjoy it very much. Often the women bring their husbands along, and we discuss various world problems. There are times, too, when some of the men and women play cards, just for pleasure, but generally we avoid card-playing. Sometimes, too, a man reads something to us from Jewish literature.

A short time ago, however, this happened: the group held a meeting at the home of a rather wealthy family. Usually at these meetings we serve tea, coffee, cake, fruit, and sometimes a snack. In some homes they like to put on a show and serve like a banquet. But at this meeting that I'm writing about, they served us only tea and store-bought egg cookies.

It was a poor table, but the women ignored it and said nothing. A friend of mine, though, made the comment, "Don't fill up on the dry cookies, because there's a roast in the oven." Some of the women took it as a joke and laughed. The hostess, visibly disturbed, began to answer that she hadn't had time to bake or buy anything. It was obvious that she was insulted by my friend's comment.

When we went home, I told my friend she shouldn't have made such a remark that insulted the hostess. I expected her to tell me she didn't mean to blurt out the comment, but she answered that she did it on purpose, because she wanted the woman to know how she felt and remember for the next time. She argued that such a wealthy woman should not serve such refreshments, because that was an insult to her guests. She claims she had the right to say something about it. But I feel she shouldn't have done it.

I would like to hear your opinion on this question, and I beg you to answer.

With thanks,
Mrs. K. M.

Answer:

The fact that the wealthy hostess served your gathering of the women's club such a poor table may be considered slightly improper. It could seem that she was treating the group as inferiors, but it could also be a fact that, for various reasons, she really had no opportunity to make the necessary preparations.

In any case, we agree with you. The woman should not have made that remark. She should realize that your meet-

ings are not just for enjoying refreshments. According to your letter, your group does quite a bit of good work, and it would be a shame for such a fine club to break up over such a trifle.

It was not a tactful remark. She should understand that among members of such a group there are some who are generous and hospitable and entertain their guests sumptuously. And there are others who are more restrained. The best thing for such a group, however, is not to make a fuss about this.

Dear Editor:

I appeal to you about an argument I am having with my dear husband.

I have a sister-in-law, my husband's older sister, who used to live in a distant city, and we used to see each other very seldom. A year ago she moved to our town to be near her daughter, who lives here. My sister-in-law is a wealthy woman, her husband earns a great deal of money, and when they moved here they bought an expensive home with costly furniture—but you can't see the furniture, because she keeps everything covered and draped.

When my husband and I come to visit, they entertain us either in the kitchen or in the cellar, which is fixed up as a basement den. I do not care to spend an evening in the kitchen or in the basement. Several times I asked my sister-in-law why she spends a lot of money on lovely furniture and then covers it up. She answered that she always did this, as long as she has been a homemaker. I must add that even in the basement one has to be careful where to stand and where to sit.

Lately when we were at their home and spent all evening sitting in the cellar, I was offended. I remarked to my sister-in-law that when, God willing, she would have grandchildren, they would never have a good time in her house because children like freedom to run around. My sister-in-law was insulted and answered me angrily that she knew how to run her own house and nobody had to give her lessons.

Now the situation is this: My husband says I insulted his sister and must apologize. But I feel I am right, and I say I can get along without going to my sister-in-law's, because I feel insulted by the way they receive us. My husband and I are arguing about this, and I would like to hear your opinion on this question.

With thanks and respect,
Mrs. Z. H.

Answer:

It is clear that it is every housekeeper's duty to keep her house clean. The cleaner a home, the pleasanter it is for the family and guests. But this only holds true when the home-maker doesn't go overboard with cleaning the rooms and polishing the furniture. There are women who are actually sick in this regard. They are constantly caught up in cleaning, and everything must shine. Not a crumb must drop anywhere. And the husband and children can go no farther than the kitchen. Such cleanliness is not a virtue, but a vice.

We believe that a house should be lived in, guests should be entertained in all rooms, and everyone should enjoy the beauty and comfort.

It seems your sister-in-law goes to further extremes. She begrudges everyone the chance to look at the attractive things in her home. She covers and hides everything so no one can cast an evil eye on it. It is truly senseless to act that way, but it is difficult to change people like that, and we feel you must stop talking to her about it.

We can imagine how you feel when they entertain you in the basement, but you must not feel insulted by it. She is not doing it to degrade you, and she certainly does not act differently in her hospitality toward other relatives and friends. You've done your part, you've let her know several times that she isn't acting properly, but since you see it doesn't help, you must ignore it from now on.

Especially for your husband's sake, you must make no more fuss about it and must not distress your sister-in-law.

Dear Editor:

For forty years I was called an "ardent socialist" who, years ago in Russia, passed out leaflets against the tsar. But since I've seen how the "free" Russia delivered all her people after the revolution, I became disillusioned with socialism.

I am writing this because I do not agree that the blame for the present-day youth crimes should be laid on the capitalistic system, on the dilapidated neighborhoods, or on broken homes. When I came here fifty-five years ago, there were capitalists and the so-called slums were even worse. I lived in Brownsville in an old house without plumbing.

Broken homes existed then also. People had to take in boarders in order to be able to pay the rent, because they did not earn hundreds of dollars a week but only four or five dollars a week. And yet, there was not so much crime then as now.

Recently I read a letter in the "Bintel Brief" from a reader who had some good thoughts about this question. She asks, and with right, what is our government doing? Instead of punishing these young criminals, they give them three meals a day and a good bed. I read recently that in Brooklyn they built a new jail that looks like a hotel.

Today's young people have everything, so they look for excitement, or better to say, they look for the easy way. And now that the government has spent billions on housing projects, what happens there? The young hoodlums destroy, rob, and rape, and respectable tenants are afraid to enter their apartments—and this is not only in the slum areas.

Our government—the politicians—when the crime rate goes up a few days in a row, announces that it will have a meeting to discuss the problem. The government should be stricter with these young criminals and not allow the city of New York to be turned into a jungle. When a boy of fifteen commits the same crime as an adult criminal, he should receive the same punishment as the adult.

With respect,
Your Long-time Reader,
Max R.

Answer:

You have touched upon a problem about which there is a lot to say and discuss. Our government can be scolded, it can be shown that not enough is being done to stop these crimes, and we can question the methods of punishment that are being used. To say, however, that nothing is being done, is wrong. Ways and means are being sought, and lately stronger punishment is being meted out to the young criminals (perhaps not yet strong enough).

Regretfully, however, not enough has been accomplished. It has been shown that the home environment has a great influence on the character development of the young. Parents play a major role in molding their children's characters, but in some cases even the most upstanding parents cannot keep their children from taking the wrong road.

Dear Friend Editor:

I ask you to give me your opinion on a question that has been bothering me quite a while. My problem is this:

I have been married to my second wife for ten years now,

and we are both in our late sixties. I have children and my wife has none. We are both well off, and when we decided to get married we agreed to make out legal papers to keep our possessions as they were, so that neither of us would have the rights to the other's assets, and we did so. It took about two years before we adjusted to our life together.

A few months ago my wife told me she wanted to make out a will and asked me how she should divide her money among her family members. She has two sisters and five brothers; her sisters are past middle age, their children all married, and they are well off—that is, they don't need any money.

I gave her my opinion on how she should divide her money among her family and, naturally, I did not mention myself. I was sure that after we had lived together so well for ten years, faithful to each other, she would certainly not forget me. But how surprised I was when by chance I read a copy of her will and found that I wasn't even mentioned. Of all my suggestions that seemed to please her when she asked for them, not one thing was done as I had advised. She left everything to her two sisters and her brothers—even some things I had bought for her were left to her sisters.

This was such a disappointment to me that I can't recover from it. Not that I need her money, but the difference between her actions and mine! I too made a will; I have children, may they be well, and yet I did not forget that she is my wife. True, she doesn't need my money, but I have provided for her for the rest of her life if I leave this world before she does. Now I feel disappointed, knowing she is not sincere. As long as she is comfortable, she is good to me. In other words, it's like a business deal.

Therefore I ask you to give me your opinion in this situation. I thank you for hearing me out and hope to see your answer in the "Bintel Brief."

I. N.

Answer:

From your letter we see that you entered your second marriage with a practical plan. You spoke quite openly with the woman about your financial positions and made sure that neither would watch the other's money, which would avoid misunderstandings.

This practical approach has helped you to live together harmoniously. Till now, everything was good and fine, and suddenly, after ten years, you feel you have a problem, and you make claims against your wife because in making out her will she did not include you. We believe you are not at all right in your claims and you're making too much of the matter.

We imagine that your wife does not expect a legacy from you, and according to your agreement, she felt she didn't have to leave you anything either. But if you felt it should be otherwise, you should have talked it over with her. As you agreed, so it should be.

We think it is not worthwhile to make a fuss about this. It would be a pity if your happy home was disturbed over this matter.

Worthy Editor:

I ask that you allow a retired man to get something off his chest.

When my dear wife died, I had to find a room for myself right away because I didn't want to stay with my children. Since it was hard to find a nice room, I took whatever I could get, but I had a lot of trouble with my landlady. She wouldn't even allow me to make a cup of coffee for myself, and she complained because I spent most of the time in the house. This disturbed me, so I decided to get married again. I met a nice woman, and we were married.

Now, when they ask me how I spend my time and how I enjoy my retirement, I answer that not I, but my wife, enjoys my retirement. I have become a "carrier" in my old age—I carry coffee to my wife in bed, I carry the laundry to the laundromat, I carry down the garbage, I carry packages from the stores—and then I spend my time in dancing, singing, and playing. To wit: my wife wants me to dance around with the vacuum cleaner, and if I refuse, I have enough to sing about. And if I try to get out of all the work, I'm playing with my life!

It's a good thing that there is a small park near our house, and when I can get away from my wife I run to the park. There I meet other men in the same situation. Here I make myself comfortable, and no one orders me here and there.

But even this is not all it should be. It happens that we get into a heated discussion about world affairs that leads to a quarrel, or suddenly it begins to rain and storm and we have to run home. So we are between the devil and the deep blue sea. Our wives are upset and drive us out of the house, and the rains drive us back in.

It's a joke—but in every joke there is some bitter truth.

> Thanks for listening,
> Your Reader,
> L. Z. from Brooklyn

Answer:

After reading your humorous letter, we thought that someone who could make light of his troubles with a smile and a joke probably doesn't have it so bad. It seems, however, that you don't have it too good either.

It is certainly a bitter thing to lose one's wife—one's life companion—and remain alone. And it is certainly not pleasant to become a boarder in a strange home in one's old age. In such cases, it is practical to marry a second time. Before taking this step, however, one has to be careful to choose the right wife, or it will not work.

You are, in a way, obligated to help your wife. But there

should be a limit. She should know that it is her duty to see to it that you are comfortable and happy. We think that it is not too late, even now, for you to let your wife know that if she goes on this way and insists on being the ruler in your home, that it can lead to a separation.

And another thing, there are enough clubs and meeting places in which retired people can spend pleasant hours every day. You should look for one in your neighborhood.

Worthy Editor:

I read the letter from a mother who wrote you that her married daughter decided to go to work to earn money for certain luxuries she wanted. I can give that young woman an example from my daughter's experience.

My daughter, too, went to work in an office a few years after her marriage—not because her husband wanted her to, or his earnings were not enough, but just because she wanted a few extra dollars to buy things for the house and prettier and more expensive things for the children. She got a job for sixty-odd dollars a week and was very happy. But she worked less than a year and gave up the job.

She found out that it doesn't pay—that she made a bad trade for the few dollars that came in. After all the expenses incurred by the job—carfare, lunches, better clothes, paying for a sitter for the children at times—she was left with about twenty-two dollars a week. And she had to pay taxes—not on the twenty-odd dollars, but on over sixty. Most important, her home was no longer a home, and nothing was ever on time. The children, under the care of a stranger, were neglected, and she had to hurry to prepare meals. Their home life, too, began to suffer when husband and wife began to have arguments.

In short, my daughter realized the whole deal was not worthwhile. She gave up her good job, and she is very happy now with her life. She realized that for a mother the most important job is to take care of her children herself and keep a decent home.

Thank you for hearing me out.

Your Reader,
Sarah

Answer:

The question of whether a married woman, a mother of children, should go to work has long been debated. In the past it was taken for granted that a married woman should stay at home to devote herself to housekeeping and raising her children. Even today there are many people who cling to the idea that a wife's duty is just to be a housewife, to have children, tend to them, and take care of her husband.

Now it is no longer a novelty that a woman who has a husband and children also holds a job. There are many women who, though they do not lack for money, are involved in careers and hold quite important positions. Those days when a woman had to fight to maintain her independence are long gone.

In the case of the woman you mention in your letter, or that of your daughter, it's a different matter. A mother who has several children at home and whose husband earns enough money does not have to go to work for the few dollars that she then spends on luxuries. If there is no one to mind the children properly, or keep the house from being neglected, it is more important for her to be home than to go out to a job.

Understandably, when there is a question of earning money for bread, and when there is not enough for necessities in the home, that's different. But even in that case, a mother should go to work only when there is someone who can take care of her children properly.

Dear Friend Editor:

Quite a while ago I wanted to write you a few words about a letter I read in the "Bintel Brief," but for various reasons I was not able to write until now.

In that letter, a mother complained that her son, a young man, was planning to marry a woman who was ten years older than he. The mother considered this a terrible tragedy and was heartbroken because she thought it a bad match. I want to say here, to that woman whom I've never met, that she should not be so worried. We had a similar tragedy, and it turned out that the bad luck became good luck.

Our youngest son, eight years ago, married a woman who was fourteen years older than he. Our oldest daughter and I tried everything; we argued with the boy that he was asking for trouble. We felt that the difference in their ages was too great. But our talk was to no avail because he was very much in love with her.

My husband, who is very pious, did not intervene; he says a match is made in heaven, and if he married her, it was a sign that the match was preordained.

Now, after eight years of marriage, they have two dear children—a seven-year-old girl, who is a fine student, and a five-year-old boy. They have a beautiful family life that couldn't be better. It is simply a pleasure to go into their home. It has turned out that our daughter-in-law is not only a beauty but also very refined and smart. If we had looked for a wife for our son, we couldn't have found a better one. And it seems that my husband is right—that matches are made in heaven.

I hope that my letter will help to assure not only that mother who wrote to you but also other mothers who have the same disappointment and heartache.

With thanks and respect,
Mrs. Z. B.

Answer:

We gladly print your letter that tells about your son who married a woman fourteen years older than he and has a happy life with her. Since it doesn't often happen that young men marry older women, such marriages are considered unusual.

We have often had occasion to print letters from parents who argue with their sons who have fallen in love with older women, and want to marry them. Most parents are against such matches. There are many reasons, but it seems to be the custom that the man be older than, or at least the same age, as his wife.

Worthy Editor:

I have been reading the *Forward* for fifty-four years now and never miss an opportunity to read the intelligent articles and the interesting works of Yiddish writers. But I must say that the "Bintel Brief" is one of the most important sections. In these letters is mirrored the life of the wide masses of humanity. Many varied community and personal problems are handled. People turn to you for advice, and the "Bintel Brief" does a good job because the answers are logical and practical.

Now it's my turn to appeal to you for an opinion. I believe that of all the letters that have been printed, my letter is the first of its kind. This is my problem:

I suffer from hallucinations or premonitions: when I drive my car, I think that if I were to get a heart attack and die, I could, God forbid, kill several people . . . or when I am on a high mountain, I think I will fall down at any moment . . . or when I am rowing on the water, I imagine that a huge wave will come up and swallow me. And often when I lie down to sleep, I begin to think that I will never wake up again.

One might think I am afraid of death, but that isn't so. In

my lifetime I've seen seventy winters, and I will not die young. One might feel that the best thing for me would be to go to a psychiatrist, but I believe that instead of going to a doctor, I would rather write to you because with your experience, you may be able to help me a great deal.

I am not an inactive man and am busy with community groups. For years I have been an active member in well-known organizations, and I fill many executive posts. People listen to me and respect me.

I would very much like to hear your opinion about such a "hang-up" or, in other words, about my eccentricity. I hope you will answer me, and I thank you for listening.

Respectfully,
H. G.

Answer:
We read your letter with interest, and we want to inform you here, at the outset, that it is not our policy to undertake the job of psychiatrist, because that is not our specialty. And though your fine letter is written clearly and factually, it is far from enough for us to analyze your situation. What you have written can be interpreted in various ways. It depends, naturally, on how deeply you are disturbed by all your dark thoughts and premonitions that some terrible accident could happen any minute.

First of all, you should realize that you are not the only one—that everyone, from time to time, is plagued with such thoughts and forebodings. We feel that people who are always troubled by such dark thoughts should seek the help of a doctor or psychiatrist. A man like you, who is healthy and active at seventy, should be thinking more of life than of accidents and death.

Worthy Editor:

As a reader of many years, I want to ask you to print my letter, before Passover if possible, because it's about the *sedorim* people conduct in their homes.

My wife and I are among the grandmothers and grandfathers who usually invite the children and grandchildren to our *sedorim* every year. For grandparents it is truly a great pleasure to have the children and grandchildren at the Passover *seder* table. But often the pleasure is mixed with sadness, because *sedorim* are no longer like they used to be. That's because the American young folks do not take them seriously. They are not interested in taking part in conducting the *seder*. And as soon as they finish eating, they leave the table and prefer to turn on the television. When there's a fight on, or a ball game, then they forget completely about the *seder*.

Understandably, this disappoints the older parents. They wear themselves out preparing for the *seder* to make sure everything is right, but the children and grandchildren don't care. It's hard to do anything about it, and it makes for a great deal of unhappiness.

I happened to talk about this with a friend of mine from another state, and he told me that in his city a group of families hold the *seder* together at the temple. The rabbi conducts the *seder*, and the families, including the children, don't leave the tables until the *seder* is over. I had an idea that it might be practical to organize similar *sedorim* all over in other temples. At such community *sedorim*, the young American children might show more interest and might take part. I believe there will be other readers who would agree with me that it would be a good thing to conduct *sedorim* together instead of in individual homes. I hope you will print my letter, and I thank you in advance.

Respectfully,
I. K.

Answer:

Passover happens to be one of the Jewish holidays that has become well established in America and has taken root in the Jewish community. The sedorim *have not been forgotten* here. Even the *wordly Jews who are not deeply religious like to observe this traditional ceremony here in America.*

Certainly many of the sedorim here are not conducted as they were in the old country. People are not as strict with children and grandchildren who are more interested in the food than in the Haggadah, and they give in to them. In many homes they are satisfied that all the family is together, enjoying a happy occasion.

But there are many, many Jewish homes in America today where the sedorim are conducted just as they were in the old country. From many homes on the first two nights of Passover you can hear the old familiar songs and melodies of the young and old as they recite and sing the Haggadah.

There are also many people who take part in community sedorim in country resorts, where they go to spend the holidays. But the greatest number of people are not interested in leaving their homes for the first two seder nights.

Dear Editor:

I beg you to forgive me for writing in English, but I cannot write Yiddish. I have a problem concerning myself and my mother, who reads the *Forward*, and I feel that your opinion could help us very much.

I am a thirty-year-old woman, not yet married. I have one brother and three sisters who have been married several years, but I have not yet met a man who pleases me. And when I do meet a man who appeals to me, I am not good enough for him. It doesn't bother me, but my mother takes it very seriously. She is upset and nags me constantly to get married.

I have a good job, I earn a good living, I have friends, and I go out on dates quite often. But as soon as I get home, no matter how late, she asks me if I have met someone who interests me!

I have thought about moving out of my parents' home, because they are quite well off and don't need the money I pay them, but I am afraid this would be worse for my mother. I don't know what to do about this, or how much longer I can stand my mother's nagging. I will thank you very much when you print my letter and state your opinion. This might calm my mother down a little.

A Daughter

Answer:

Don't think your mother is the only one so anxious to see her daughter married. Most mothers of daughters are no different. Mothers are ready to marry off their daughters even before they grow out of their baby shoes. They start looking for husbands for them and talking about the future to their girls when they are still young. And if it happens that a girl is in no hurry to make a match and gets into her twenties, it's a real trauma.

You should not be angry with your mother about this, because she means you no harm. You must try, gently, to calm her and explain that today a girl your age is still considered young and has the same opportunities as a twenty-year-old to find a young man who will love her wholeheartedly.

It may be that you are a bit too fussy, but your mother should understand that you can't marry just anyone—that he should, after all, appeal to you. She has no right to nag you and should not be eating her heart out, because you surely will find your destined man.

Your mother should realize that putting pressure on you, urging you to take a husband, could have a reverse effect on you and actually prevent you from marrying. There's no reason for you to hurry. You are independent, you live a good life, and neither you nor your mother should be worried. Girls like

you who go out in society and enjoy being with people are
seldom left single. It's just a matter of time and patience. The
day will come when you will please your mother with an
announcement that you have found Mr. Right.

Dear Friend Editor:

I come to you about an argument I am having with my
wife. She has taken it into her head that I didn't do the right
thing by her cousin and her husband—or better said, I didn't
do right by their dog.

My wife invited her cousins to our house for lunch. They
came and brought their big dog along. When we were ready to
sit down to the table, they took a chair and, without saying
anything or asking permission, sat the dog on it. And when the
food was served, they put some on a plate for the dog, as
though he were another human being.

This got me so angry that I left the table and ate my lunch
in the kitchen. Well, the cousins were so insulted by my action
that they told my wife they would never come to our house
again.

This doesn't bother me, but I think that instead of my
eating in the kitchen, I should have thrown the dog out. I am
very upset with my wife, however, who hasn't stopped nagging me, although both our married children keep telling her I
was right.

Anyway, my wife gives me no rest. The arguments don't
stop, and more than once I think it will come to a point where
I will have to leave her. I am not a young man, and after a
day's work I want to come home and relax and not have to
listen to her nagging.

I ask you to print my letter and also tell me who was right.
I hope you will answer me right away.

Respectfully,
Harry B.

Answer:

If you could get involved in a serious argument over such a nonsensical thing, neither of you is right, in our opinion. Instead of leaving the table, you should have been frank and told your wife's cousins to take the dog outside or, at least, take him to the kitchen and give him his food there. You certainly had the right to tell them that only humans ate at your table. If you had done this, it might not have caused a quarrel.

You didn't commit a crime by going into the kitchen. Your wife's cousins should have realized at the moment you left the table that they had done something wrong. And your wife shouldn't have made such an issue of the whole thing.

Worthy Editor:

I have a serious problem, and I ask you to give me some advice on how to handle it.

I have only one sister here. She is angry with me, and I am sick over it. I would like to make up with her, but she wants nothing to do with me. My sister was rescued from the Holocaust and came here to me after the war. I helped her with a few hundred dollars and was happy to have her with me, because I am very lonely.

I received my sister as a brother should, though I myself am not a rich man, but she didn't appreciate it. After she stayed with me eight days she left, and I didn't know where she went. A long time later I found out her address, and I started asking her to come back. Just at that time I had to undergo an operation, and since I am all alone I wanted to have her near me. But she estranged herself from me altogether.

My sister lives in New York, and I live in another city. When I discovered her address I began to write to her, but she sent back my letters unopened, and she doesn't want to write me even a few words.

I never did my sister any harm, and I cannot understand why she hates me so. Why is this coming to me? When she came over from the other side I did everything possible for her. I was happy when she came, and I thought I would have a close person near me, but she has disappointed me bitterly.

I simply want to know how she is, is she healthy, does she have enough to live on? But I don't know what to do about it, and I beg you to help me with advice.

Respectfully,
G. D.

Answer:

It happens that misunderstandings occur between new immigrants and their American relatives—misunderstandings that can lead to serious quarrels and rifts. Sometimes the proper tolerance between the newcomers and the old settlers is missing. Though they are of the same flesh and blood, they have been apart for many years and become estranged. It also happens that the Americans look down on their "green" brother or sister, and this keeps them from drawing close.

Also there's no lack of complaints against the Americans because they didn't give enough assistance to their relatives who saved themselves and came to America with high hopes. Many of those who were rescued came here with incurable wounds. They lived through a great deal, and though they escaped the murderer's hands, they are spiritually and physically broken. And for someone who is so sick, whatever you do is not good enough.

Your letter is not explicit enough for us to guess why your sister is so angry with you. We imagine something must have happened between you both. It makes no sense for your sister, who was left alone and was drawn to come to her only brother, to get angry and leave without any excuse. Maybe there is a reason, but you didn't mention it.

But since you are so eager to make up with your sister, it is advisable that you find someone to help you convince her that she shouldn't remain estranged from you.

Dear Editor:

I turn to you for advice about my bitter situation, and I hope that my letter will serve as a warning to others to avoid acting foolishly as I did.

A year after I came to America I married a very nice girl, and with the few dollars I had, I opened a small store. This was some thirty-odd years ago. My wife and I worked very hard and slowly became successful. Although my wife worked very hard in the store, she also was a good housewife and raised our two children, who are now married. My wife also took good care of my father, who lived with us until the day he died.

In this way we lived a happy and peaceful life for over thirty years, but I didn't appreciate it as I should have, and a few years ago I did a terrible thing. I met a young woman who was divorced and let her turn my head. She was about thirty and I was over sixty. This didn't keep me from becoming involved with her. I spent a lot of time with her and felt that in her company, I was young again.

The young woman bewitched me, and the end was that I divorced my wife and married her. For my family and close friends, this was a blow. They reviled me and said I had lost my mind.

My wife, however, didn't say a bad word to me, although she suffered a lot. I gave up the business, gave my wife half of our savings, and went off with my young wife. We traveled around for a few months and then settled in another city, so I wouldn't be too close to my family. Before a year was up, however, our love burned itself out. We both began to realize that we were not a pair. She quickly lost interest in me, and I had no more love for her. She cost me a lot, and I left her.

Now I am alone and a broken man. I cannot forgive myself for having so deeply hurt my wife—the mother of my children—with whom I had such a good life. It is done and past, and now I wonder what I can do.

I would be the happiest man if everything I've done were no more than a dream. I wouldn't even think about the money if I could wake up and find myself with my dear wife in the small store we opened so many years ago. I don't know how I can return to my family, but this is now my only wish. The question is—what to do now? Maybe you can give me some advice.

I thank you for hearing me out, and I beg you to answer me.

With respect,
I. A.

Answer:

If you had turned to us for advice before you did such a terrible thing, we could have told you it wouldn't work. You were, however, so drunk with love for the young woman that you lost your senses and, like a blind man, ran straight into the fire.

It is not hard to imagine what your wife and children went through, how much pain and shame you caused them, when you were enthralled in a love that quickly burned itself out. Then you didn't want to think about anything and didn't care that you trampled on the feelings of your wife and children. Now that you have sobered up, you realize what a disaster you caused.

You are looking for ways to get back to your first wife and children. We know it won't be easy to find a way, because you sinned grievously against them. But it may be that in time they will be able to forgive you.

It may be advisable for you to find someone in your family to talk to your wife and children and tell them how much

you regret having left them, and in time you can write them
yourself. Time may heal the wounds you inflicted, and they
may be able to forgive you.

Dear Friend Editor:

My husband and I are married over thirty years, and we always had a quiet, happy life. I don't say that we never had disagreements, but we never had any serious quarrels or became angry with each other. When we sometimes had words, we made up quickly and everything was fine again.

In the past few years, since our daughters married and went to live their own lives, my husband has begun to pick on me. I take care of the house just as I did before, and I see to it that he has everything he needs. He doesn't say that I'm a bad housekeeper, God forbid, and he is very happy with the meals I prepare for him. I even get compliments from him for being a good housewife, but lately he complains that I dress up too much.

He can't stand the fact that I like to get dressed up and often shouts at me when he thinks I've used too much powder and lipstick. Not long ago he got very angry with me because of this. We were going to a party, and it took me longer than usual to get dressed and ready. When I was finally ready to leave, he was very upset and began to yell that I had put on too much makeup and he didn't like the dress I had on. The result was that he made me so angry, I didn't want to go with him. I washed my face, and he went to the party by himself.

We were angry for a while. He complained to the children about me—said it took me too long to get dressed and that I used makeup like an actress who is about to go onstage.

I don't deny that I like to dress nicely when we have to go out. I always felt this way, and since I am not so young anymore it takes me a little longer to cover the wrinkles and to try to look younger. I am over fifty and my husband is in his sixties. I cannot stand my husband's complaints, and very often, when we have to go somewhere, I tell him to go by himself because I know what he will say when I take my time getting dressed. He would like me to wash my face, throw on any dress, and be ready in minutes. However, I cannot do things this way.

I want to know, am I really so wrong in my actions? I ask you to express your opinion about my problem.

Respectfully,
Mrs. B. F.

Answer:
Not long ago we had a letter from a man who complained because his wife let herself go and never wore a nice dress, but your case is just the opposite. Your husband complains that you spend too much time on clothes and makeup.

Of course, it is very important for a woman to be well dressed when she goes out with her husband, or by herself. And certainly her husband should be glad that she keeps herself clean and neat. But if the wife goes overboard and spends too much time on clothes, it isn't good.

It may be that your husband isn't altogether wrong. Perhaps you do spend too much time on clothes, or do use too much makeup. It is hard for us to judge in this instance because we haven't heard your husband's side. It may be he exaggerates a bit, but since you always got along so well together, maybe he isn't picking on you without cause.

It isn't a serious problem in any case. You must realize that small incidents can develop into serious disagreements, and you should see to it that this doesn't happen. You should both compromise and try to find a middle ground. Your daughters should be able to help you in this. They can tell you if you're overdoing things. You had a good life with your husband for many years, and you shouldn't let such minor disagreements disturb your family life.

Worthy Editor:

I come to you with a problem that concerns my sister, and as a reader of the *Forward* I ask you to express your opinion of this matter.

About two years ago my sister lost her husband. Her children, who are very good to her, settled her in a lovely home and gave her enough to live on. My sister is seventy-three years old now, but she does not consider herself an old woman. Her face shows that she is over seventy, but she doesn't want to admit it, may she be well.

About two years ago she went to Florida, where she became acquainted with a man in his seventies and fell in love. I can tell you, I have never before seen people of their age so in love. They kiss in public, and the man keeps complimenting her, calls her "darling" and other pet names.

Since my sister's lover doesn't live in the same city as she, he comes to her every weekend, and they stay together from Friday to Sunday night. My sister prepares all kinds of good food and drink for him. She gives him cooked fish, roasted chicken, and more to take home so he won't have to go to a restaurant. Her lover is no great sport—he doesn't pay for anything.

But my sister doesn't care. She is so happy that she's not alone and has someone to keep her company. This has been going on for two years now. I spoke to my sister a few times and asked her how much longer she will let him delude her with his sweet talk. I also asked her whether she wasn't ashamed to take her lover into her home a few days each week. I tell her she's not behaving decently, and she answers that she can't help herself, because he claims to believe in "free love."

My sister would surely like to marry him, but when he hears that kind of talk, he doesn't come to her at all. When he doesn't show up, she gets so unhappy, as if her world were coming to an end. She explains that she feels very lonely when he doesn't come.

My sister has often taken him to meet her children, but he has never introduced her to his own, who are also married. Her children are already asking her how much longer she's going to go out with this "young man." Since he's retired, my sister would be willing to take him into her home, and there would be no question of money if they married. We would like to hear your opinion and your advice on this matter. Thank you.

Respectfully,
A. M.

Answer:

We live in a free country, and everyone can lead his life as he pleases. However, you have the right to disagree with your sister's actions.

It is no novelty that an older woman or an older man can fall in love. We know of people your sister's age who married for love and are very happy. But before and after their wedding, they behaved as older people should.

We must come to the conclusion that your sister took a wrong step from the beginning. Just for the sake of her children and family, she should not have become so submissive and yielded to this man. She should have maintained her dignity. It is unheard of that a decent woman, who is most likely a grandmother, should walk such a crooked path. Her answer, that she feels lonely without this man, is just an idle excuse. No, your sister cannot justify her actions with this excuse. Her family has reason to scold her for embarrassing them with her way of life.

If the "young man" is sincerely in love with her, he should give in to her desire and marry her. If he refuses, that should be a sign that he is just taking advantage of her, and she must end the relationship.

Dear Friend Editor:

As a reader of the *Forward* I turn to you with a matter that affects me, and I ask that you answer me in the "Bintel Brief."

It is about my nephew, who is married to a non-Jewish woman with whom he has three children—one son and two daughters. His wife and he are not religious, and when they were married, they didn't go to a rabbi or a priest. She is a very nice woman and keeps close to her husband's family.

When their son was born, to please my sister, they had him circumcised. Now he is ten years old, and they want to give him a Jewish education. My nephew, because of the family, wants his son to be *bar mitzvah,* and his Christian wife is not against it.

My nephew went to the synagogue in his neighborhood, told the rabbi the situation, and asked that his son be enrolled in the Hebrew school that they have there. To his amazement, however, the rabbi informed him that they cannot accept his son because his mother is not Jewish and never converted to Judaism.

This was a complete surprise to my nephew. To be truthful, I ask the same question: Where is justice? I cannot understand why the rabbi acted thus. A father wants his son to learn something about *Yiddishkeit* so he can be *bar mitzvah,* and the rabbi is against it.

I turn to you for advice about this and ask you to answer me as soon as possible. I want to know if the rabbi has the right to act so. I would also like to hear from other parents who are in the same situation as my nephew.

I thank you in advance for your answer.

With respect,
Mrs. L. L.

Answer:

Your nephew is not the first to encounter this difficulty. To our regret, this is one of the problems that arise in mixed marriages.

There are many knotty situations that arise when it comes to the education of children of mixed marriages. Your nephew was certain that his son would be readily accepted in the Talmud Torah, and here the rabbi closed the door to him. He, therefore, has complaints against the rabbi, and you also ask, "Where is Justice?" The answer is that the rabbi didn't act according to his own feelings, or justice, but according to Jewish law.

In the "Bintel Brief" we can't get involved in problems that deal with Jewish law or religious interpretation. We do allow ourselves to explain to you here that your nephew's son, even though he was circumcised, is not considered a Jew simply because his mother is not Jewish. According to Jewish law, the children in every case, and also in a mixed marriage, are the mother's. This means that if the mother were Jewish and the father a non-Jew, the children are considered to be Jewish and would be accepted in a Talmud Torah.

We wonder why the rabbi didn't explain this to your nephew. In any case, your nephew should go to see another rabbi in order to learn all the details.

Dear Editor:

I know you can't help me, but I must tell someone about how my children have disappointed me.

I can tell you that I and my deceased wife devoted our lives to our children. I worked very hard to earn enough for them, and there were times that my wife didn't eat or sleep because of them. We saw to it that they got a good upbringing, that they studied, but they never appreciated it. Now that I am elderly, they treat me like a stranger.

My children, when they were already independent, took money from me and involved me in businesses that brought me only trouble. They always did only what was good for them and never considered me.

Now that I am old and without my life's companion, I am lonely and alone. When my wife died, they did come to me and I thought they really sympathized with me in my sorrow, and I drew closer to them. It turned out, however, that they didn't care about me, just about my money that they came, ostensibly, to borrow from me. They took as much money as they could from me and then didn't show themselves again. I now have a lot of time to think about their treatment of me, and I see that they were the smart ones and I remained the fool.

I will be very grateful if you will print my letter and give me your answer.

Respectfully,
I. S.

Answer:

Although your letter doesn't give any details, it moved us deeply. We don't know how many children you have, nor do we know exactly what they took from you. We also do not know what kind of business they got you involved in, but we imagine that you have good reason to be so bitter about them. It may be that your children have an answer to your complaints about them, but they are wrong in having become estranged from you now that you are old and alone.

Since we don't know anything about your conversations with your children, nor how much money they still owe you, it is hard to judge in this instance. We feel, however, that in spite of all your complaints about them, you should find a way of getting together and talking to them. You might do this with the help of family or good friends. It may be that you can straighten things out with them. You are, after all, of the same flesh and blood, and it is certainly worthwhile to try to get closer to them.

Dear Friend Editor:

I turn to you with my problem, and I hope you will answer me soon.

I am from Poland and came to America as a young girl over forty years ago. Here I married and settled down. I have a very nice life with my dear husband; we raised fine children, and we already have grandchildren.

From the days that I came to America, I always hoped that sometime I would be able to bring over my whole family and that we could live here together. My hope turned to ashes, however, because the Nazis with the help of the Poles destroyed my entire family; only my youngest brother was saved. When I left for America, he was a little boy.

Since the horrible news reached me, that of my large family only one brother remained alive, I am a broken person. I cannot recover from this terrible tragedy that befell me and the whole Jewish people. I cannot forget this. Of course, I helped my brother and was ready to bring him to America. But after being liberated he decided to go to Israel. There he married and slowly made a life for himself in the Jewish land and is now doing quite well.

Lately he has written that he would like to come to America with his wife (they have no children) to be near me. They make a nice living in Israel, but my brother wants to be closer to me, and I wonder how to handle this. My brother is now in his late forties; he doesn't have any trade, and my husband thinks it would be hard for him, at this age, to start over again.

Therefore, I would like to hear your opinion. What shall I write my brother? My dear husband is not against my sending them tickets. We are not wealthy, but we can afford to do this. The question is—will I be doing the right thing for them? Of course, I'd like to have my only living brother near me. This would be a great solace for me. However, I meet many newcomers here who are not happy and are angry with their relatives for talking them into coming to America.

I ask you to answer me in the "Bintel Brief," and I thank you in advance.

With respect,
Mrs. G. B.

Answer:

We sympathize with you in your tragedy, which is, as you say, the tragedy of the whole Jewish race. Many years have passed since the extermination of the six million Jews by the German murderers, but the pain and the anguish are still fresh and cannot be forgotten.

Certainly it would be a good thing for you to have your one remaining brother near you. Since he has been living in Israel for many years and has made a life for himself there, it is questionable whether he will, at this age, be able to find something to do here.

From your letter, it is clear that you would really like to have your brother close to you. Since, however, you and your husband see the thing clearly, it is natural that you are in no hurry to convince your brother to give up everything in Israel to come to America. It is possible that your brother and his wife who are not so young will find it hard to acclimate to the life here, even though they will have your help. You must write them about this because they must take it into consideration.

America is still the land of opportunity, but not for everyone. There are many immigrants who made good lives for themselves here. But there are also others who couldn't adjust to the life—they don't like anything and complain about their relatives who brought them to this country.

Your brother and sister-in-law should know about this, and you must write about it. The best thing would be that they come here first for a visit. Let them come, and then you can all come to a decision.

Dear Friend Editor:

I am a woman of seventy, and as an old reader of the *Forward* I want to get something off my chest. Not long ago I became a widow for the second time, and my life is bitter.

I lost my first husband when I was in my forties. My husband was not much older than I, and we lived happily together. I helped him in his business in order to make it easier for him. We had a good life, but then I lost him.

When I was left alone my friends began to talk to me about marrying again, but I waited a few years. I can tell you that it was very hard for me to be alone, and when, in time, I met a man who appealed to me, I decided to marry a second time.

He was a widower with two children, but he was a fine, decent man and I got along very well with him and his children. I was like a mother to his children, and when they married, we both led them to the altar. The children lived with us for a short while after they were married. It was a good life, and I got into the habit of going to the station every evening to meet my husband when he came from work. Even in the worst weather, I went out to meet him.

I lived with my husband many years and then, four months ago, I lost him too and I am left all alone. Now in my loneliness I think of my husband constantly, and in the evening about the time he used to come home, I still go out to the station. I stand there hoping he will come home from work, wait a while, have a good cry, and then walk home alone. It makes me feel better when I have a good cry, but I know I should stop going to the station to wait for my deceased husband. The question is—how can I do this?

I ask you to please answer my letter.

With thanks and respect,
Mrs. J. S.

Answer:

It is evident that you were very attached to your husband and that you miss him very much. The wound is still fresh, and it is difficult for you to accept the fact that he is no longer among the living. You think of him constantly, you see him clearly, and you believe that he will be coming home.

We imagine how bitter your life must be—to be left alone in your older years without your dear friend—and we sympathize with you. But sad to say, there is nothing that can be done about this. This is the way of life—those who leave us cannot be brought back. You must take yourself in hand and face the reality.

You don't say anything in your letter about your children or your husband's children, but we hope that you get along well with them and are in close contact. It is most important for you to be with people now.

Worthy Editor:

I come to you with my problem, which could lead to the breaking up of our peaceful home. I am a man in my thirties, my wife is a few years younger than I, and we lead a good life. My wife devotes herself to our two young children and the housekeeping, and I am, as usual, the provider.

I work hard all day, and when I come home, I'm very tired. I need rest, but the thing is that I never get enough sleep. My wife got into the habit of sleeping on her back, and as soon as she shuts her eyes, she starts to snore so loudly it seems as if the walls tremble. As soon as she falls asleep she begins to give "concerts," blowing and whistling with such shrill tones they could waken even the dead.

Her snoring makes me so nervous at times that I poke her to wake her up. Then she opens her eyes and complains that I do not let her sleep. She gets mad at me and continues with her nightly music, while I am forced to listen.

What can I do? Give me some advice. I thank you for your answer.

The Sleepless Man

Answer:

Just recently we had occasion to read in a newspaper about a woman who took her husband to court and asked for a divorce because he snored. But the judge declared that such a minor thing did not constitute grounds for a divorce, and he dismissed the case. If your wife is devoted to you, however, she should take this minor thing quite seriously and seek a way to cease her nocturnal concerts. First of all, a person can break the habit of sleeping on her back, and secondly, she should see a doctor because it is possible that she could be helped.

Dear Editor:

I am already forty-two years old and was married only two years ago. It may be that because I am not American-born, it was hard for me to find a suitable wife. When I came to America I was already a grown man, and a cousin of mine warned me to be careful of the American girls because they always want to boss their husbands.

I took my time choosing, but when I saw my hair start to turn gray and since I didn't want to be an old bachelor, I decided to hurry it up and married a girl who was in the country only six years.

It didn't take me long to find out that she is the type of person who wants everything her way. The first week after we were married she insisted that I give her everything I earned. I am not even allowed to open my weekly salary envelope. She takes all the money and then gives me what I need for the week. She rules me with an iron hand, though she is not American-born, and she is constantly ordering me about. I come home from work tired, and she orders me around like an errand boy. I have to go shopping for her, and often she makes me go back to change things two and three times if they don't please her.

I must admit that she takes good care of me and sees to it that I am always dressed well, but she yells at me and has even warned me that she will slap me if I don't obey her. I am twelve years older, but she bosses me around as if she were older than I.

She is a good housekeeper, but she cooks only what she likes. I don't feel comfortable in my own home and I don't know what to do. I think maybe I should leave her before we have a child. I cannot come to a decision, and I ask you to give me some advice.

With respect,
H. Z.

Answer:

When we read your letter we realized that you were the kind of man who is a weakling, whose wife can make a nothing of him. We were surprised that you even wrote to us, because usually such men who are weak in character, and let their wives make slaves of them, keep quiet. They can't protest and are ashamed to tell how they are dictated to by their wives. But you tell all.

It is hard to give advice to a man like you. You got yourself into this mess, and now you ask for help to get you out. It is questionable, however, if you can be helped. We have the feeling that even though you don't like the fact that your wife has made a slave of you, you are not ready to be freed. We have the feeling that in spite of all your troubles, you are still in love with your wife.

If you don't love your wife, we cannot understand why you put up with her. And if you do love her, you must insist

*that she treat you with respect. If you don't have the strength
to do this, you should rid yourself of her and become a free
man.*

Dear Friend Editor:

We have two daughters and a son and they, as well as our
grandchildren, are very dear to us. Our greatest pleasure is to
be with all of them. Lately, however, we are disturbed about
our daughter-in-law and our son. We visited them often, as we
did our daughters and sons-in-law, and enjoyed being with
them and their two children, who are three and five years old.
Our daughter-in-law was never too friendly toward us, but we
overlooked a lot.

Not long ago when we were visiting them, our daughter-
in-law suddenly told us we shouldn't come so often to spend
time with our grandchildren and that we shouldn't visit them
on weekends when they have company. I didn't understand
what she meant, but she explained that since the children
were growing up, she didn't want them to learn from us to
speak English with a Yiddish accent. Our daughter-in-law also
wasn't ashamed to tell us that we didn't fit in with their American friends.

We are not American-born (we came to this country over
forty years ago), and it is true that our speech is not perfect,
but we were very hurt by our daughter-in-law's remarks. I
answered her immediately and said that when we were younger we had no time to learn English as it is spoken in high
society because we had to work very hard to raise a husband
for her with a college degree. My husband worked enough
overtime hours in order to send our son to college and make
him a professional.

My husband wouldn't let me continue my discussion with

our daughter-in-law, and we left in anger and went home. Next day our son called, and I thought he would tell me his wife had been wrong, but he said he had discussed it with his wife and they decided it would be best if we visited them only every other week on a specified day. I was so upset, I hung up on him in the middle of our conversation, and we haven't been there for several weeks.

Now, I ask you, is this right? Should children act like this? What can we do however, when we love the grandchildren so? We are brokenhearted, and we wonder if we have to abide by the "rules" set up by our daughter-in-law? I ask you to answer as soon as possible.

With deepest thanks,
Grandma and Grandpa

Answer:

Your son deserves to be censured more than your daughter-in-law. He should never have allowed his wife to set a definite time when you can visit with your grandchildren, so they should not, heaven forbid, learn to speak English with your Yiddish accent.

It is natural that you should be hurt by your daughter-in-law's remarks that you don't fit in with their friends who are "real" Americans. Your daughter-in-law's attitude is ridiculous and certainly not in the American tradition. Many well-known personalities who hold important posts in government, in cultural organizations, and in the arts are children of immigrant parents who didn't speak English well, but this didn't keep them from attaining success in their chosen fields. And these successful people are not ashamed of their parents who came from overseas. They often speak with pride of their parents and grandparents, who enriched their lives.

We think someone in your family should explain this to your son and daughter-in-law and show them how wrong they are. We would also suggest that you go to visit your

*grandchildren and your son and daughter-in-law less fre-
quently than before, because to continue being angry with
them won't help the situation and will do you no good.*

Worthy Editor:

I am a very busy man because I work in my little store
from morning to night, but I decided to write to you because I
am having trouble with my wife.

I am a man of fifty-odd years. My wife is a few years
younger, and we have already married off our only child. But I
still work hard and never get out to see the world. I do not
achieve great miracles, but in the last few years I've started
saving money for my old age because it will come soon
enough. I shouldn't complain because in the old days one had
to stay in such a store till midnight, and many people had to
be carried on credit because there was much poverty. But it's
still not too easy.

My problem, however, is that when my wife is with me in
the store I have trouble with her. It is customary that when a
shopper comes in, you should be friendly, sometimes kid
around a little, tell a joke, but when I talk to a woman this
way, or give her a smile, my wife gives me a hard time. She
refuses to understand that this is business. It appears to her
that I flirt with the women and make a fool of myself. She
thinks modern times are different and you don't have to be too
friendly with the customers, but it's not so.

Lately, it's worse than ever. In the past she didn't watch
me so closely, but now it's so bad I feel like selling the business. We quarrel often and I don't know what to do.

I beg you to answer in the "Bintel Brief," which my wife
reads every day.

With thanks,
Your Reader, S. N.

Answer:

*It is difficult for us to understand what is going on be-
tween you and your wife. You've lived together for many
years, and just now your wife has begun to complain that you
smile and flirt too much with the young pretty women who
are your customers. Something is wrong here, and we think
it's one of two things: Maybe your wife has lost her faith in
you lately for some reason, or she has begun to listen to idle
gossip.*

*If you do not feel guilty, the best thing would be for you to
make every effort to convince your wife that your only inten-
tion with your friendliness toward the women is to keep them
as customers. She should realize herself that people now are
just like they were years ago. She should know that men as
well as women do not like to go into a store where the sales-
man has a sour face and looks at them angrily.*

*If you have no influence on her, your daughter (or your
son) should talk to her. Yes, it is generally required that one be
friendly toward people, and your wife should be pleased that,
in spite of long hours and hard work, you still have the spirit
to be friendly, to smile, and to joke.*

Dear Editor:

I am a widow who has suffered much in life and is now
alone and lonely. I have been alone for three years, and these
years without my husband have been the saddest of my life.
Even when he was sick, chained to his bed, it was better for
me than it is now. I am sixty-seven years old and already I live
only with the past. When night comes I feel the emptiness of
my home, and I talk to the shadows on the wall.

If you think I have no one, you are mistaken. I have a big
album filled with pictures of my five children and grandchildren. I have them, but only on paper. Thank God that my

dear husband, whom I can't forget, left me with a small income, that I can also earn a little myself, and that I do not have to take anything from my children.

It's not an idle saying that "one mother can support ten children, but ten children can't support one mother." My children are all married and live comfortably, but they have no time for mother. They come seldom, but I believed that at least one son, one daughter, or at least a grandchild would come to me on the Sunday of Mother's Day. All day I sat at home by the window till it got dark, but no one came.

Since they are my children, after all, and I love them in spite of everything, that evening of Mother's Day I made the house bright and visited with my absent children in my album. I looked at the pictures of their childhood days when my husband and I were young, wiped away a few tears, and went to bed.

I thank you for giving me this chance to unburden my heart a little.

A Mama

Answer:

We have read with compassion your moving letter in which you describe your loneliness, and about your children who didn't visit you, even on Mother's Day. It is hard to understand why they have become so estranged from you but it is possible that you, too, are partly guilty. Whatever has happened, they deserve to be scolded severely for their heartlessness. It does happen, however, that children grow away from their parents because they are from two different worlds.

Whatever the case may be, it would be advisable for you to try to retain the ties with your children. A mother must be able to overlook her children's faults, and if they don't come to you, then from time to time you should go to them. You needn't wait for an invitation. Perhaps your efforts would make it possible to draw them closer to you.

Dear Editor:

My husband and I have been in America for eighteen years, but my sister-in-law, who came to this country over forty years ago, still considers us greenhorns. Although my husband's sister was good to us at the beginning and helped us a great deal, the fact that she and her husband have been lucky and became wealthy makes her believe she's wiser and knows more than everybody else. From the first day we came to the country she began to teach us how to behave and how to live. I'd like to note here that my husband and I had a good education, and she had none, not in the old country nor here. But her diamonds and bank books give her a lot of *chutzpah*.

My husband and I couldn't stand her talk, her boasting and bragging, and we were delighted when we were able to acclimate and break away from her. My husband is in business, we live in our own home, and our son has his college degree. A short time ago our daughter was married. Yet my husband's sister still considers us greenhorns. We've overlooked a lot since she is my husband's sister, but we've had enough to bear.

I would like to remark that according to our figures, we owe my sister-in-law and brother-in-law nothing. The money we borrowed from them when we first came to this country has long since been repaid to the penny, and my husband worked in their business to pay for their help.

During the past years we seldom went to visit our in-laws because they simply alienated us. My husband goes there alone occasionally, uninvited, to see how they are.

When we married off our daughter a short time ago, our in-laws were among the first ones we invited to the wedding. But they did not come. They sent a worthless gift that cost a few measly dollars, and a short cold note explaining that they couldn't come because they were going to Florida. We learned later that they really left two weeks after our daughter's wedding. Now my husband says he doesn't want anything to do with his sister any more. Isn't he right? We want to hear your opinion.

> Thank you for your answer,
> Mrs. E. T.

Answer:
We have had occasion previously to print letters in which people rescued from the Holocaust complain about their American relatives. In most cases, the complaints are justified, and we believe your accusations against your sister-in-law, who considers herself superior to you, are not unfounded. We do not know what transpired between you and your sister-in-law in the course of the past years. But they did you a great wrong when they did not attend your daughter's wedding.

You close your letter with the statement that your husband wants no more contact with his sister, but it is not easy for him to break off with her. Even when they are angry with each other there is still love in their hearts. We believe his sister feels the same, but she certainly deserves a scolding for the way she has behaved.

We believe you should not break off relations entirely with the only relatives you have in this country.

Dear Editor:

I have a serious problem and I hope you will help me with your advice. I will explain briefly what it's about.

I came from a small town in Poland, and I married there. But four years after my wedding, World War II broke out, and in the great Holocaust we were separated from each other. We had no children and everyone ran wherever he could. For years I didn't hear from my husband, and when I returned to my hometown after the war, I didn't find him there. I found no one from my family in the town; everything was gone up in smoke and and fire, and I was told everyone had perished.

In time I married another man because I was certain that my first husband was dead. Later it turned out that he was alive. He unexpectedly returned, as if from the grave. When he learned that I had married he said nothing but left quietly, and I didn't know where he went.

I lived quite peacefully with my second husband, but after eight years together he died. Since I had relatives in America, I came here with their help after my husband's death. Here I accidentally met my first husband. It didn't take long, and we were married again.

We adopted two children and we lived happily. But in time my husband started quarreling with me over what happened in the past. It got so bad he left the house. He sends money for me and the children, but he doesn't come. He is very bitter, and I wonder if he isn't right. He is devoted to the children and I would like to have him back home.

Meanwhile I have heard that he is going out with another woman, and this bothers me. What can I do in my present state? Do I have the right to force my husband to come back to me and the children? I beg you, give me your suggestion how to handle this.

I thank you, and I beg you to answer soon.

Respectfully,
Ashamed

Answer:

You are not the only one to suffer from the aftershock of that terrible time when the bloodthirsty German hordes and their allies annihilated six million Jews. It is difficult for us to mediate in such a tangled problem that arose from that chaotic time. We feel we have no right to scold people for their past actions. Nor is it our place to judge, from the view-

point of Jewish law, whether you had the right to marry a second time. We do not engage in deciding religious questions; for that there are rabbis. We must therefore refrain from pointing out which of you is right.

From your letter it is evident you want to make peace with your husband. This would certainly be good for you and especially for your adopted children. But you cannot force your husband to come home, because force will not accomplish anything. You can force him by legal means to support his wife and children, but you cannot tell him that he must live with you.

Dear Editor:

I wanted to write this letter to you a few months ago, but I kept putting it off because I thought my complaining about my daughter-in-law would be interpreted as my being a bad mother-in-law. I have, thank goodness, three daughters-in-law and get along very well with two of them, but my youngest son's wife is not close to us.

Our youngest son was married two years ago, and I was very happy with the match. I was generous to my new daughter-in-law, as I had always been with my other son's wives, but she was never too friendly to me. I overlooked a lot because I know my son is very much in love with her.

She doesn't act like other young wives and doesn't spend too much time on housekeeping. She gets her husband to take her out to restaurants several times a week, and since she doesn't have a child, she goes out most afternoons with her friends to look for bargains in the stores.

This wouldn't be so bad, but several months ago she ran into an old friend she used to go out with before she met my son. This man came to her home unexpectedly one evening when I happened to be there. She was delighted to see him and introduced him to her husband. My son received him coolly, but she paid no attention and invited her friend to come again for supper.

As I understand it, my son was not pleased about his coming, because he never came to her home again in the evening. Some time ago I learned that he has visited her in the afternoon when she is alone at home. I've been told that she was seen in a restaurant with her friend, which means that she is meeting him in secret.

I am very aggravated that she is exchanging my son for her old boyfriend, and I can't keep quiet about this. My son, who is in love with her, knows nothing about it, and I haven't told him anything yet because I don't want to upset him. It is also a question of whether he'll believe it.

I think I've written enough for you to understand the situation, and I ask that you tell me how to handle it.

With sincere thanks,
Mrs. S. V.

Answer:

Your accusation against your daughter-in-law is a serious one, but since your letter is not too explicit and we have no details, it is hard for us to say anything about this delicate situation.

It may be that your daughter-in-law has rediscovered her old love, because such a thing is possible. But what you've told us is not enough to prove that she is betraying your son. That she's been seen with her friend in restaurants, and entertains him in her home when her husband isn't there, is not enough proof that your accusations are valid.

It seems that you yourself are not convinced it is true, and you only have your suspicions. We therefore advise you not to exaggerate this and not to tell your son anything about it until you are one hundred percent sure it is true. Because of silly gossip, your son's good marriage can be destroyed.

Dear Friend Editor:

I know my problem is not serious, but I want to hear your opinion and I ask you to answer me in the "Bintel Brief."

My husband and I do not consider ourselves old, even though we already have grown grandchildren. We belong to several organizations, we have many friends, and we go out often. My husband still works part time, and we have a good life. We got along well together all these years and never had any complaints against each other.

Some months ago, I had an accident—I fell and broke my hand and was in a cast for several weeks. I also suffered many bruises when I fell, and had to stay in bed a long time. My husband spent the days at home with me, and he took over the housekeeping. From my bed, I taught him how to cook a meal and what to do in the kitchen—and this he enjoyed.

He was very good to me—didn't let me do a thing—and became a good cook. He even prepared a dinner all by himself for our daughter and her two sons when they came to visit us. I was certainly grateful to him for his help while I was unable to move. I felt his devotion every moment, but the end result was not good.

Cooking has become a hobby for my husband, and although I have long since completely recovered, I cannot get him out of the kitchen. He has really become quite a good cook, but which housewife likes a man in her kitchen? In addition, after he cooks, I have enough work to clean up the kitchen.

When I drive him out of the kitchen in a nice way, he gets angry. He is insulted because he feels that I don't think much of his cooking. I would like to hear your opinion about this. Am I really wrong in not wanting my husband underfoot in my kitchen?

I hope you will answer me soon and I thank you for your attention.

Respectfully,
Mrs. C. S.

*   *   *

Answer:

Your problem is really not serious, and you shouldn't make an issue of it. Your husband served you well and showed his devotion when you were unable to do things yourself, and if cooking has become a hobby that he enjoys, you should allow him this pleasure.

There are many women who are very happy with this type of husband who enjoys cooking and housework. They encourage their husbands by praising their cooking. It appears that you are a housewife who cannot tolerate it when her husband dons an apron and gets busy in the kitchen.

You shouldn't make a tragedy of this, however. Since your husband has developed a love of cooking, you shouldn't drive him out of the kitchen completely. You see that cooking has become important to him, therefore you shouldn't deprive him of his hobby. It would be a good idea to let him have the kitchen one day a week and see what he can accomplish as chef. He must understand, however, that the kitchen is the wife's province, not the husband's.

Worthy Editor:

I hope that you will not mind that I bother you with a trivial question, and that you will answer my letter.

I will make it short: my husband, to whom I've been married some thirty-odd years, has been squabbling with me. The situation is this:

I am a woman over fifty, and since I was always busy with our four children and the house, I never bothered too much with fancy clothes. But my husband always liked to dress well. We raised two daughters and two sons who are now all independent, and we always lived peacefully. My husband always liked to flirt with other women, and he's no different now. I always ignored it. I realized it was his nature, and he meant no harm in paying attention to other women.

Since our children are no longer with us and we are now alone in the house, I have very little housekeeping to do, and I have plenty of time to go out with my husband and with my married daughters. My daughters are trying to talk me into dressing better, and even bought several dresses for me. They practically forced me to start dressing up like my husband does.

My husband seemed pleased that I was dressing better. But when my younger daughter took me to the beauty parlor and had me get my hair tinted black as it used to be before it turned gray, he didn't like it. When I got home from the beauty parlor he stared at me with a hurt look, then began to shout that I shouldn't have done it.

His shouting made me answer him back that more than one of the women he flirted with had dyed hair. He didn't like what I said, and since then he's been angry with me. I want to know if I really committed a crime when I dyed my gray hair.

Thank you for your answer.

Mrs. M. G.

Answer:

Your husband, who always liked to dress up, should know that nowadays it's nothing new when a woman of your age has her hair dyed. Older women do it, and it's become a natural thing to do. It may be, though, that your husband is angry because you let your daughter talk you into it without his knowledge. It's really too bad that you didn't talk it over with him before you decided to do away with the traces of gray.

But since the deed is done, and since you and your daughter thought it would be a pleasant surprise for your husband, he shouldn't make a big deal of it. If it's important to him that you keep the gray instead of black, it doesn't pay to let that disturb the peace in your home. It must not cause a serious quarrel between you.

Worthy Editor:

I turn to you regarding a discussion I had with my husband, and I ask you to tell us your opinion as to which of us is right. I would like to remark here that it is not in our nature to argue. We've been married over thirty years, and we get along very well.

We are a large family and we often go to visit each other. A short time ago when we went to see one of our relatives, I feel that my husband did not behave properly. A couple gave a party on their return from a trip to Israel and Europe, and there was a gathering of many relatives and friends. Since my relative's husband has long practiced the hobby of taking pictures, he brought home from this trip plenty of pictures he had taken with his movie camera. When we gathered at the party, he set up his equipment and began to show the movie. It was as if we sat in a theater, and at first everyone enjoyed it. The pictures were beautiful, but it took too long. Since my husband has no patience to sit still for long, and because he was tired after a day's work, after about ten minutes he began to yawn aloud and soon he began to snore. I kept giving him a poke in the side with my elbow, but it didn't help. He woke up, then fell asleep again.

My husband could hardly wait till they would turn the lights on again in the dining room and serve something to eat and drink. He announced in a loud voice that he was tired and we should go home. I could hardly restrain him. Looking at him, some of the others began to yawn and doze, so my relative's husband cut his show short. I could see immediately that he was angry and glared at my husband. Then as the coffee was served, my husband started to joke that when he went to the movies alone, he could sleep well, but when he watched home movies, his wife kept nudging him and waking him.

When we got home I had words with my husband over

this, but he insisted that the host had a nerve to keep us so
long in the dark and show so many pictures. He thinks he's
right. Therefore I would like to hear your opinion on the subject, and I will thank you if you answer me soon.

With respect,

Mrs. L. D.

Answer:

*From your letter we understand that your host, who is
very enthusiastic about his hobby, entertained everyone too
much with his movies of his travels. He wanted to show you
all the places he and his wife visited, and most likely he also
wanted you to see how well he photographed them. But it
seems he went too far and showed too much, and that was
wrong on his part.*

*Your relative and her husband surely meant well. They
wanted, in a nice way, to share with you the impressions and
pleasures they experienced during their trip. They probably
didn't know that your husband has no patience, that he's such
a great sleeper, and that his yawning would infect others.*

*Your husband should consider this. He should have apolo-
gized and gone into another room. Instead of joking about it,
which was not called for, he could have explained to his host
during the refreshments that he had had a hard day and
couldn't keep his eyes open. But it's not so serious a matter
that you should quarrel about it. At the first opportunity you
should explain this to your relative and her husband, and
then it won't lead to a serious quarrel.*

Dear Editor:

I am writing you this letter about my older sister, with
whom I always got along well, but lately we're having a dis-
agreement. This is because I am not pleased with her actions

and have told her so. She knows well that when I tell her
something, it's for her own good, but she won't listen.

My sister is almost seventy, and I am about two years
younger. We have a younger brother, and we always stuck
together faithfully. Now it's like this: my sister became a
widow four years ago, and two years after her husband's
death she married again. Her three children have long been
independent, and when her husband died she was very de-
spondent. She was left well off, but it was hard for her to be
alone, and her children talked her into marrying again.

My sister's second husband is a decent man, and they get
along quite well. But from the time when, with the help of
friends, she began to look for a match for herself, she started
providing men for other widows. She doesn't do it for money,
but she has become a real matchmaker, and wherever she goes
she tries to match up widows with widowers. She has managed to bring together several couples in this manner.

I don't approve of this, but when we get together with
friends, no matter what the conversation is, she starts asking
which of the men are not married. It's gone so far that they
jokingly call her "The Matchmaker," and I can't stand it. But
when I tell her she shouldn't busy herself with this, she gets
angry.

Now I question whether I should draw away from my
sister a bit. I will be thankful to you if you give me an idea on
how to handle this.

                                    Your friend,
                                    Mrs. H. S.

Answer:

If you always got along well with your sister and stayed
together faithfully, you must not now, in your elderly years,
even think of becoming estranged. You have no reason to be
angry with your sister. It should not even begin to bother you
if her new hobby is involved with matchmaking. She most
likely gets satisfaction when now and then she succeeds in
getting two lonely people together. Don't make any waves

about this, and don't make yourself believe that your sister is
demeaning herself. If anyone jests about it, it is certainly with
good will and not making fun of her.

In general, you should not try to dictate to your older
sister how to behave. She's already a woman of ripe old age
with a lot of experience. You have mentioned in your letter
that she is respected in the circles you frequent, so how can
you imagine they're laughing at her?

In short, you must not quarrel with your sister over her
hobby. You would be committing a serious error against her
and yourself too if you alienate yourself from her.

Worthy Friend Editor:

Not long ago I read in the "Bintel Brief" complaints about
benevolent societies and I hope you will permit me to say a
few words on the question.

Since I am active in a society, I have something to say
about all the complaints that are heard. Believe me, the active
members of societies today are not to be envied. In former
times members of societies were young people and new members kept joining. But now? Now, no new members come, and
the old ones grow older. What was the old adage? "Young ones
can die, but old ones must die." Under such conditions, it's
very hard to protect an organization from falling apart.

The writer of that letter remarked that he didn't have the
desire to go to meetings because they were not conducted like
they used to be. He expressed the feeling that everything always has to be as the officers want. He thinks that the society
is run by the newcomers, who do not want to consider the
opinions of the older people. This writer doesn't want to understand that what was good for the society fifty years ago is
not good today. And if the majority of members agree on
something, you can't do just as you please. He should be
thankful to the present-day members, who guard what was

built up years ago. As an old member, he must know that every society has its rules and regulations. It may that if the old members saw to it that their children became members of the society they had built everything would be different now.

Finally, I want to say that those who are still active in the society should be blessed, because if not for them, the society would fall apart like a house of cards.

Respectfully,
P. S.

Answer:

We gladly print your letter about societies and how difficult it is now to carry on their work. The old members grow older and fewer, new ones do not join, and under these circumstances difficulties arise. Most of the societies are no longer what they once were, but that has nothing to do with the leadership.

We must agree that in some societies that have dwindled in membership, all is not in order. It even happens that because of the disorder, some members have to appeal to the Jewish Court.

Dear Friend Editor:

We've lived through a lot, and now we face another problem.

My husband and I are not religious, but we lead a traditional Jewish life. Therefore, it was a blow for us when our daughter, without telling us, married a non-Jew. When she came to tell us what she had done, she kept promising us that she and her husband, who is a learned man, planned to keep some of the Jewish tradition in their home. We were angry with her, but since we didn't want to become estranged from our daughter, we accepted the inevitable.

Our daughter told us that they had had a civil wedding and didn't go to a rabbi or a priest. Now the question is, what will happen to their children? My daughter is pregnant and says if she has a son, she wants to name him for my late father and wants to have him circumcised. Her husband is a good man and has no objections, but the question is—will this be possible?

Not long ago I was at my sister's home and I was told that since my daughter's husband is not Jewish, they cannot make a *brith*. We don't know if this is so, but we, and especially our daughter, are very upset. She hopes to have a son and wants him to be named for her grandfather, who was a religious man and whom she loved dearly. Our non-Jewish son-in-law is not religious, but he loves our daughter very much and wants to do everything he can to make her happy.

I ask you not to delay giving us your answer because the time is short.

With thanks and respect,
B. R.

Answer:

Though the "Bintel Brief" column doesn't print letters about this type of problem, we will make an exception in your case, which shows the confusion in Jewish life today.

We don't give advice on religious matters because, first, we don't know all the details, and second, there are, thank goodness, enough rabbis here who can handle these questions. Therefore, it would be advisable for you to consult a rabbi about this. Finally, we want to note that many children of mixed marriages are very disturbed when they grow up, because when they are asked whether they are Jews or Christians, they don't know what to answer.

The Seventies

Worthy Editor:

I am writing this letter for a friend of mine who reads and speaks Yiddish but cannot write. It involves a family problem, and she will be very thankful if you will answer her in the "Bintel Brief."

My friend has been married a long time; she and her husband are middle-aged, and they live very happily together. I would like to mention that she is attractive and intelligent. Lately, though, she is upset over something that I consider a trifle. The thing is this: a few months ago a woman of her husband's hometown, also middle-aged but unmarried, came to the house. She came to ask them to translate a Yiddish letter she had received from her relatives in Russia. My friend's husband did it gladly, and she thanked him warmly.

Since then, the woman has become a regular visitor. She comes with a Yiddish letter, and my friend's husband gladly reads it for her. But she has formed the habit of kissing him when she comes and when she leaves. He made no secret of this and told his wife that the woman kissed him, and she didn't take it seriously. But once she noticed, from another room, how they kissed, and she was disturbed and asked him about it after the woman left. Her discussion put him in an uncomfortable position, and he answered her that it was not his fault, that it was always the woman who made the advance to kiss him and he didn't want to insult her. It came to a quarrel between my friend and her husband, and she told him quite frankly that he could translate the letters the woman brought, but he should not kiss her. The man argues, though, that the woman means nothing to him, but he can't push her away because that would be an insult to her.

Now my friend would like to know how to handle this, and I ask you to state your opinion.

Mrs. A. V.

Answer:

We feel that what is going on between your friend and her husband is a trifle. It appears she has no grounds to be upset over the fact that the woman kisses her husband when she comes and when she goes. The woman may not be a close friend of the husband's, but she feels close because they come from the same town. It may also be that she is lonely and wants to feel at home with the couple. We imagine it doesn't occur to her that his wife sees any harm in it.

We are quite sure that the woman is innocent and hasn't the least idea that your friend is jealous when she kisses her husband. A kiss between a man and woman these days is a natural greeting, and your friend should not make a big deal out of it.

Dear Editor:

My husband and I have been in America many years now, and we have been married over forty years. I come from Orthodox parents and my husband has belonged to a socialist organization since his youth, but we lead a traditional Jewish life. He does a great deal for Israel. I keep a kosher kitchen, and we observe all the holidays. The city we live in has a large

Jewish population, and we had the opportunity to give our children a good Jewish education. Our eldest daughter is married to a rabbi of a Conservative temple.

Some years ago we brought my husband's two nieces over to America, and we treated them like our own children. They adjusted well to the city we live in, and in time married here. With my husband's help they went into business, and they have accomplished a great deal. They have beautiful, talented children, and we derive much pleasure from them.

But lately we are upset by their actions. The nieces come from a fine, religious family and we expected that both of them would bring up their children in the Jewish tradition. But it has turned out differently. They became Americanized and their children, who are already in high school, know nothing of Judaism. They made fancy *bar mitzvahs* for their two sons, but the boys didn't even know their *alef-beth*, and the receptions were held in nonkosher halls.

My husband and I talked to them many times about this and even warned them that their children would bring home gentile daughters-in-law and sons-in-law, but our words had no effect. My husband's distress about their attitude has alienated him from his nieces. But I argue with him that cutting himself off from them will only make the situation worse. We always told them that it was important to send the children to a *Talmud Torah* or to a modern Jewish school, but they argued that the children had enough work at school and it would be too hard for them. They are very much opposed to mixed marriages, but they are doing nothing to prevent this from happening to them.

I ask you to answer in the "Bintel Brief." Thank you.
Respectfully,
Mrs. F. H.

Answer:
The issue in your letter is not new to us. Unfortunately, there are many of these Jewish parents who neglect giving their children a Jewish upbringing. Many of them give the

*same excuse as your nieces. That is, they do not want to over-
burden the children by sending them to Jewish schools in the
afternoons, which might keep them from getting good marks
in the English school. For quite a few of these parents it's good
enough for their young sons to prepare for their bar mitzvahs
by learning the prayers from a record for the ritual and part
of the haftorah. The most important thing for them is to have
a fancy affair.*

*There are plenty of parents who force their children to
learn to play the piano, the violin, or whatnot. But there's no
time to give them a decent upbringing. Your nieces and their
friends do have the right to bring up their children as they
please, but you and your husband must explain to them over
and over again that they are committing a grievous wrong
against their sons and daughters when they do not give them
a Jewish upbringing. They must be made to understand that
training children in the Jewish tradition absolutely does not
interfere with their secular education. Actually, the Jewish
lore will expand their knowledge.*

Dear Friend Editor:

I am now in such a predicament that I must talk it out
with someone.

It is about our one and only daughter, from whom we
have plenty of trouble. It has happened because she matured
very early and at fifteen was already going out on dates. We
tried to reason with her in a good way, then in anger, but
couldn't accomplish anything with her. At twenty-one she
married a man without telling us. She knew we'd be against it
because the man was the same age as her father. We didn't
even know she was going out with this man, and when she
brought him home and announced to us that they had been
married in a rabbi's study, I almost fainted. She said that she
loved him, but I think the fact that he was wealthy and bought

her expensive gifts meant a lot to her. A year after they were married, she gave birth to a daughter—a beautiful child—and the years passed.

Now it is twelve years since their marriage, and our daughter has blossomed like a flower—she looks very young and beautiful. Her husband, however, just went through a serious operation and has aged a great deal. He lost all his hair and looks like an old man. After his illness he became very nervous, and he is ashamed to go out with his young, beautiful wife and their daughter. People think he is my daughter's father—the grandfather, not the father, of their child. This bothers him, and they do not have a good home life now. Summer and winter are not a pair.

Our daughter has to stand for a lot from her husband now. He doesn't want to go out with her socially, and if she goes out alone, he doesn't like it. It has gone so far that she is talking about a divorce. She wants to start with a separation but I tell her she shouldn't do it, although I am not certain that she should stay with this man.

Therefore I want to hear your opinion. I will be very thankful if you answer me as soon as possible in the "Bintel Brief."

Mrs. S. B.

Answer:

We don't know all the details about your daughter's marriage to this man who is twenty-odd years older than she, and we know little about their family life. But it seems there are enough reasons for them to think about a separation.

It is not unusual for such marriages to end in divorce. Your daughter was really too young to marry this man. In the first years of their marriage she was in love with him, but in time there was an awakening. In addition, there is the fact that her husband, after the operation, aged and became very nervous. She realized that it is no good, and that they would probably have to get a divorce.

There is a possibility that they may be able to solve their

misunderstandings and avoid the necessity of breaking up
their home, and so it is good that you discourage her from
separating. It would also be advisable for your daughter to
consult a marriage counselor before she takes the step of
breaking up her marriage.

Dear Editor:
    We are about to marry off our oldest daughter, and we
wonder what kind of wedding to arrange. We have, thank
goodness, three daughters who are all grown up, and it seems
that in less than three years' time we will have three weddings. Our daughters are all pretty and talented, and the young
men grab them up when they are very young.
    The oldest, whom we will lead to the altar this summer,
has a very fine young man. Both he and our daughter are
working, and they earn enough to live very comfortably. My
husband is in business but we haven't saved any fortunes.
However, I wanted to make a big wedding and invite all our
relatives and friends. This is our first child to be married, and I
wanted everything to be lavish. My dear husband doesn't
agree with me. He says that we should make it simpler because this is our oldest child and we still have two more
daughters. He feels if we make a big wedding for this daughter, we will have to do the same for the other two.
    It is true that such a wedding runs into thousands of dol-
lars, but other people in our circumstances who are far from
rich borrow money to make a splash. My husband says that he
doesn't have to show off for anyone, and doesn't want to pose
as a rich man when he isn't. Our daughter and her young man
haven't made any demands and will be happy with any wedding arrangements we make, but we still can't decide what to
do.
    Our future son-in-law's parents are also not rich, and they
have hinted to me that we shouldn't make a big wedding but

instead give the young couple the money to furnish their new home. I feel, however, that we should make a big wedding and invite all our friends who invited us to the nice weddings they made for their children. Therefore we want to hear your opinion.

I ask you to answer me in the "Bintel Brief," and I thank you in advance.

With respect,
Mrs. M. K.

Answer:

Our answer is that it is not necessary to play the role of a wealthy man when one is not. This means that we agree with your husband. One shouldn't go into debt just to show off for others. You don't have to do as others do—rent tuxedos, top hats, and gowns that they never in their lives wore.

We think that you should listen to your husband and together with him, your daughter, and her young man plan a nice but simple wedding that fits your circumstances. At times one makes a big wedding because the bride and groom as well as the in-laws insist on it, but in your case you have no such problem, and there is no need to go into debt. Also, you shouldn't forget that you have two more daughters to marry off.

Dear Editor:

I write this letter with my husband's permission, and I beg you to answer me. We have been married well over twenty years, and we have two children, a twenty-one-year-old daughter and a son who is still in high school. My husband always earned a good living, and we always got along well together.

But lately we've had a difference of opinion over our

daughter, whom we love dearly. She is a good girl and we've never complained about her. She graduated from high school, had two years of college, and for over a year now she's held a fine job and earns a good salary.

Our children always had everything they wanted. Our daughter had all the luxuries from us, and now that she is earning money, she spends it all on herself. At the beginning we did not expect her to contribute money toward the house, but after several months went by and she didn't mention it, my husband felt badly. We are not millionaires, but we can get along without her few dollars. My husbands feels, however, that a girl who is earning money should be self-supporting.

Our daughter has all the comforts of home. I prepare the finest meals for her, and she has her own lovely room. She said she wants to save some money, and has a bank book, but when she had a few hundred dollars, she went away on a vacation and withdrew everything she had saved.

It would be good if she would give me a definite sum every week. I would save the money for her, and she would spend less on things she doesn't need. My husband insisted that I talk to her about this. I obeyed him and told her, but she ignored me. Now I am afraid that when my husband talks to her a quarrel will ensue, and it could go so far that she would move out on her own. I know my husband doesn't mean any harm, but I beg him to wait and say nothing now. What is your opinion?

With thanks and respect,
Mrs. H. R.

Answer:

A girl who is already twenty-one years of age and earns a good salary should understand that it's time for her to act like a self-sufficient person. It doesn't matter whether you need your daughter's few dollars or not. But it is important that she should realize that she should not be dependent on her parents forever.

It seems that from childhood on, your daughter had the idea that everything was coming to her and her parents could never refuse her anything. She never learned that in time she would have to support herself. We must come to the conclusion that she now behaves as she does because you spoiled her.

We agree with your husband that she should give part of her earnings to you. It doesn't matter how much. She must show that she is becoming self-sufficient and supporting herself.

Dear Friend Editor:

After fifty years of reading the *Forward,* including the "Bintel Brief," from which one learns a lot about various problems, I have to turn to you for advice.

It deals with my life with my husband, with whom I have lived for fifty years and always worked very hard with in our small business. He worked hard also, but his whole life was devoted to making money. Money was more important to him than his wife or children. I worked with him but I wasn't allowed to go to the cash register, because he watched to see that I didn't take an extra quarter after he gave me the few dollars to run the house. In his miserliness he saved thousands of dollars, and even if he should live another seventy-five years he would not be able to spend all the money he has saved. This money, that is due in part to my hard work, is in his name only.

This man doesn't belong to any organizations, doesn't give a penny to Israel or to any other cause, and never buys any gifts for me or the children. Why did I stay with him all these years? The answer is that we had children, and because of them, I overlooked everything. Our children, thank God, grew up to be respectable individuals. They are now planning a big party to celebrate our fiftieth wedding anniversary, and I question whether I should allow it. I feel that their father, who made their mother's life miserable, doesn't deserve it.

I want to hear your opinion and I ask you to answer me soon.

With thanks and respect,
Mrs. D. S.

Answer:

Though we don't know what your husband has to say about your complaints against him, we imagine that your bitterness toward him is not unjustified. It is certainly no small thing to live for fifty years with a man who counts every penny he gives his wife and begrudges her anything.

It may be that you exaggerate a bit when you write about your husband's stinginess. If everything is really as you describe, then he certainly deserves to be severely censured. But we must say that you are partly to blame for your troubles. You should never have allowed the money you both worked so hard for to be only in your husband's name.

Why haven't your children interfered until now and seen to it that their father treated their mother better? To try for a more harmonious life for their parents is more important than arranging a big anniversary party. If your children have their hearts set on making such a party, it would be good for them to postpone it for a year, and in this year to try to convince their father to turn over a new leaf and start to live like a human being. If they can bring some harmony into your lives, then they will have something to celebrate at your golden wedding anniversary.

Worthy Editor:

I am brokenhearted about the tragedy that happened to me, and although I have two children, I am very lonely. Several months ago I lost my devoted husband to whom I had been married over forty years, and I have cried my eyes out. We lived a good life, though we were not wealthy, but we never complained. We both worked hard and saw to it that our two sons got a good education and never wanted for anything.

With my husband's death, my own life has been shortened. I am more or less assured of a small income and don't have to ask anyone for help. But what kind of a life can it be without my dear husband? I have been left alone in my apartment, and when evening comes, I find myself talking to the shadows on the wall.

I have two fine sons who live quite far from me, but I go to visit them often, looking for solace from them and my grandchildren. I can't control myself and I cry a lot when I'm there, and my sons and daughters-in-law scold me and say I have to stop mourning. They want me to be like them and stop grieving. One of my daughters-in-law even told me it had a bad effect on her children when they saw their grandmother always sad and tearful. This attitude bothers me a lot, and it seems that I should stop going to visit them.

I cannot say that my sons and daughters-in-law are bad to me, but they recovered from their sorrow quickly and expect me to do the same. My life is very bitter, and I am writing to you because I have to pour my heart out to someone.

I hope you will answer me and I thank you in advance.

With respect,
Mrs. N. S.

Answer:

It is not hard for us to understand your situation, and we feel for you in your sorrow. We think, however, that you should have no complaints about your sons and daughters-

in-law. They are young people who are busy building their family life, and though they surely loved their father and father-in-law, they weren't affected by the tragedy as strongly as you.

Certainly they should show you more sympathy, but you must understand that they don't want to hurt you. They want to lift you out of your sorrow, and therefore you shouldn't draw away from them. It must certainly be a solace to spend time with your sons and their families.

You must also take yourself in hand and realize that you have to go on with your life without your husband. You must find an interest in something. You might find it worthwhile to get involved in social work, since this would be interesting and take your mind off yourself.

Worthy Editor:

As a reader of the *Forward*, I turn to you to ask you to be so kind as to help me with a problem. I will state briefly what it is about.

I've been a widower for several years, and though I was not quite sixty when my wife died, I had the idea that I would not marry a second time. I gave up my apartment and rented a room from a couple I had known before. At that time their bachelor son was still living with them. The man and his wife were several years younger than I, and they were friendly to me.

A year and a half ago the husband died, and I stayed on there. A few months ago their son fell in love and will soon be married. The woman hasn't told me that I must find another lodging, but I can understand that it is not proper for her to continue living with a stranger. Therefore, I spoke to the woman and let her know that I'll move out soon. She heard me out and let me know that we had plenty of time to discuss it.

I've really been quite comfortable here, but I realize I should start looking for another room. When it was close to the time for her son's wedding, I asked her if she knew of anyone who had a room for rent. She smiled and answered that I had quite a nice room in her house. Then she became earnest and said, "You need not and you cannot move away from me, because I won't let you." In short, the woman declared that she wanted me to marry her, and that I couldn't refuse. I don't know whether she's after my small amount of money or not, but she told me in no uncertain terms that she wouldn't let me go, as if I had promised that I would marry her. But I have never spoken to her about marriage.

My question is this: can she take me to court and sue me? I would be thankful if you could advise me what to do.

> Anxiously,
> A Reader from the Bronx

Answer:

We are not sure that you have given us all the details in your letter, since we cannot believe that this woman, whose home you are living in, has attached herself to you in this manner, so that you would have to marry her. While reading your letter, we have a notion that it is possible that the widow has, as they say, a "mortgage" on you—that her demands have some sort of basis. The fact that you are disturbed strengthens our feeling.

If you feel, however, that you have no obligations to this woman, you have no cause to be worried and you need not take her threats seriously. If you do not feel guilty, you must move out as soon as possible.

The woman has cause for complaint only if she can prove

*you had a very close relationship and that you made prom-
ises to her. If this is so, you must talk the situation over with a
lawyer.*

Worthy Editor:

I don't know how to handle the situation that has come up
between us and I am turning to you for advice.

My husband and I are both elderly people. We have already married off our two sons and our only daughter, and we
live in peace and quiet. My husband is planning to retire soon
because first, he is not in the best of health, second, he is
already past sixty-five when people stop working, and third,
we have saved enough to be able to live very comfortably.

We spend a lot of time with our children and grandchildren, and this gives us a great deal of pleasure. Our daughter has two children, little girls who are quiet as doves, and
from time to time she leaves them with us for a day. Our older
son has two grown-up boys, but they don't visit us much. Our
second son also has two boys—eight and ten years old. They
are spoiled and very wild, and when my daughter-in-law
brings them to us for a weekend they tire me out. There is,
however, no greater pleasure for me than to spend time with
them.

My dear husband, however, has no patience with the two
boys. He says they make him nervous, and he scolds my son
and daughter-in-law, telling them they should be stricter with
their sons. Now the thing is this: Our son and daughter-in-law
are planning a trip to Israel for two weeks, and it seems that
they will leave the two boys with us during that time.

I am ready to have the boys stay with us but my husband
is against it. First, he says, they can afford to send the children
to a summer camp. Second, he feels it will be too hard for me,

and his nerves can't take it. My husband wants them to make suitable arrangements for the boys now and not rely on us. I think that this may cause a quarrel.

I feel that it would not be too hard for me to have the children for two weeks, and that we shouldn't make an issue of this. My husband insists, however, that he wants to talk to our son and daughter-in-law and very politely offer to give them part of the money to send the boys to camp.

We want to hear your opinion, and I thank you in advance for your answer.

With respect,
Mrs. L. N.

Answer:

It is very good to have a close relationship with your children and to help them out when they are already on their own. It is also pleasant for grandmothers and grandfathers to have their grandchildren spend a day or a weekend with them. This does not mean, however, that married children should take advantage of their parents. It is really too much for you to have the two boys with you for two weeks since they are so spoiled. Your son and daughter-in-law know that you are no longer young and do not have the strength or patience for these two boys. If they don't realize this themselves, they should be told in a nice way.

We feel that your husband is absolutely right. Everything has to be within limits, and when children try to take advantage they should be made aware of the situation. The idea of sending them to a summer camp is a good one. It is good for them to stay with you for a day, or to sleep over one night, but to be with you for two full weeks is not practical.

Dear Editor:

I very often read letters from mothers-in-law who have complaints about their daughters-in-law and keep defending their sons, but in my case it's the opposite. I am complaining about my son because he doesn't treat his wife right.

The thing is this: My son has been married ten years and they have two lovely children—seven and five years old. He was lucky in his marriage because his wife is very sweet and easy to get along with. My son has an important job and earns a good salary. My daughter-in-law is a good housekeeper and is more careful with a dollar than my son. She doesn't look for luxuries and lives very modestly. My son, however, likes to show off—to take long vacations and to buy a new car every year. For this, however, he needs more money than he earns.

Of late he has come up with the idea that his wife should get an office job and that I should take care of the children when she is at work. His plan, however, doesn't appeal to me or his wife. My daughter-in-law thinks that the children are still too young to be without her all day, and feels that she doesn't have to go to work.

I have talked to my son and told him that he should forget about having his wife go to work because her place is now at home with the children. What will happen later, time will tell. My son doesn't want to understand that it is more important for her to be a housewife and a mother to her children than to go to work and earn money that he will fritter away.

I don't have the right to interfere, but I am distressed that they have already had some arguments about this. My son can take very good care of his family with what he earns. I want to hear your opinion about this question, and I thank you in advance for your answer.

With respect,
Mrs. Z. V.

Answer:

It is not unusual for women, also mothers of young children, to go to work even though they are not in need. These are women who prefer a career to staying at home, being a housewife, and taking care of their children. They do this not because their husbands ask them to, but because they prefer it. In many cases the husbands are against their going to work because they want to be the sole support of their family.

In the case of your daughter-in-law, it's the opposite. She wants to stay at home but her husband is trying to have her get a job. If it is as you say, he shouldn't force her to leave the children alone all day and go to work. If one must for economic reasons, it's something else. If, however, there is enough income and your daughter-in-law is happy with what she has, she shouldn't be forced to take a job. It is also not right for your son to expect you to take care of his children five days a week.

You can speak very openly about this to your son. Also his wife should explain to him that if she went away from home every day, her mind would not be on her job, but on her children.

Dear Friend Editor:

I am a grandfather over eighty, and I have a lot of aggravation when I see the behavior of my dear grandchildren.

I have one son who lives far away, and I have had the great "pleasure" of having his son married in a church. I also have children who are professionals who live not far from New York, and they belong to a synagogue. My grandson who received a Jewish education led the congregation in prayer at his *bar mitzvah* and also read the *haftorah* very well. When I was there for Sabbath, the sister of the *bar mitzvah* lit the Sabbath candles Friday evening and he made the *kiddush*.

Everything was fine, and his mother and father thought that he was growing up to be a rabbi. But it turned out differently. As time passed, he changed completely. He let his hair grow long, and he goes around with a bunch of Christians. He doesn't listen to his parents anymore but does just what he wants to. His sister is no different from him now. She is going out with a Christian boy, and it seems that, though there are over four hundred Jewish families in the city, they cannot find any Jewish friends.

The rabbi and the active members of the congregation should do something about this. They should arrange meetings and entertainment for the Jewish youth so that they could spend time together. I am very worried about this.

I see what is going on and I cannot keep quiet. It is hard for me to observe the actions of the youth in these crazy times. I cannot rest and therefore I am writing to you about this. I hope you will answer me.

Respectfully,
A. F.

Answer:

You have touched upon a problem about which we have received many letters of late. You are not the only grandfather who is pained to see how these stormy times have caused an upheaval in the lives of many of today's young people. It has gone so far that parents have very little influence over their children, who are becoming estranged.

We understand very well how hurt you were that one of your grandchildren was married in a church, and that two other grandchildren seem to be following in his footsteps. It is certainly not the "pleasure" that you expected to have from your grandchildren. But you must understand that you are not the only one who is going through this. To our regret, the number of mixed marriages is increasing, and not just one family suffers from this.

We don't know in what circles your two grandchildren spend their time. We imagine that in a city of four hundred Jewish families, there must be a Jewish social life. There must also be a youth group in a Jewish Center or synagogue that keeps the Jewish youth together. It would be very practical, however, if the rabbi and members of the congregation would devote more time to the younger generation.

Dear Editor:

I need advice from an experienced person. And who can be more experienced in such a matter than you, worthy Editor of the "Bintel Brief"? This is the issue:

My wife and I have been married for sixty-five years, which means that we are both over eighty. We lived a good life and raised a fine family. We have, God bless them, one son, two daughters, and five grandchildren. I am a tailor by trade, and all my life I worked in the shops. Through the years I managed to save quite a good sum of money for the days when I would no longer be able to work, so that we won't have to look for help.

Since we are now old folks, my wife had an idea that we should divide our money among our children and grandchildren while we are still alive. But I do not agree with my wife's plan. True, we are living on borrowed time, but we are still living. Besides that, I think that when the time comes, in a hundred and twenty years, if one of us outlives the other, it will be hard to remain alone in the house.

We get along quite well with our children, but we agreed that we do not want to live with them. Therefore I believe that when the times comes when my wife, or I, remain alone, there should be a good place prepared where one could live out his final years in peace. It may be that we might, while we are both alive, give up our home and have to find a suitable place. And for that you need money.

As you see, our ideas differ. Therefore we want to hear your opinion. I hope you will answer soon and I thank you very much.

Respectfully,
I. K.

Answer:

We don't know exactly how much or what you possess. You also do not mention in your letter whether your children are in need of money. If your children are in want and you have enough, it would not be wrong for you to help them. It is no novelty that parents help out their grown-up children who need it. But older people must always keep in mind that they should take care of themselves first.

Parents who have complete trust in their children do not hesitate to hand over to their heirs their business and their money. But from letters we receive, we find that many of them regret it. Therefore we feel it is our duty to advise your wife to give up her plan to divide your money now among your children. She must realize that you are more practical. But if your children need your help, and if you feel you have more than enough, you could help them. For the entire inheritance, they can wait a hundred and twenty years when they will receive it all in your will, which you have, no doubt, made.

Dear Editor:

My husband and I are now elderly, and we lead a quiet, happy family life. We raised our three children in a truly Jewish tradition, since my husband is a religious man. Our children are long since married, and they have, thank God, lovely families. But now we are facing a problem.

We have a son, who is the oldest, and two daughters. Our

daughters married men who carry on the Jewish tradition. In their homes the Sabbath is observed, as are the holy days, and our daughters keep kosher kitchens. But with my son, who attended a *yeshiva* for a few years after his *bar mitzvah*, things are different. The reason is that he married a woman who doesn't believe in *kashruth*.

Now, our son and daughter-in-law are preparing to marry off their only daughter, and though they know my husband, the grandfather of the bride, is a religious man, they're planning the affair in a nonkosher place. I hurried to speak to our son and to our daughter-in-law—who is making all the arrangements—but they pay no attention. She thinks highly of this nonkosher place and won't listen to us.

I don't want to see a quarrel come from this, so I have been begging my husband not to make trouble and to go to the wedding. I also told him we could arrange to have two kosher meals brought in for us, but he won't listen. He's upset with his son, even more than with his daughter-in-law, because he agrees with everything she says. He can't understand why they want to feed the guests nonkosher meat. It seems to my husband that since they're arranging such an affair, it's not important to them that we come to the wedding.

Our daughters told us that if we do not go to the affair, they too will not accept the invitation, and this will lead to a real fight. I don't know how to handle it, and I ask you for your opinion.

With thanks and anxiety,
Mrs. E. M.

Answer:

We do not understand the conduct of your son and daughter-in-law. When they are marrying off their only child, they should most certainly consider the immediate family, who are rightfully the most important guests. And who can be closer than the parents, the sisters, and the brothers-in-law? Without them, the affair has no feeling and no taste.

No one can find fault with your husband and your daughters for not wanting to go to the wedding. It's as your husband says: if your son and daughter-in-law don't take into account the fact that you are kosher, it's a sign that they don't care whether the closest relatives come to the wedding.

We hope, however, that both the bride and her parents will realize that this is not the right way to act, and will decide to hold the wedding in a kosher place. The daughter-in-law, in this case, should not have the final say.

Dear Editor:

My husband and I are blessed with three daughters, all of whom have been married a long time. From the older two we have lots of joy, but the youngest, who is thirty years old, didn't do well in her choice of a husband. In the beginning it seemed a good match because he came from a fine family and earned a good salary. But these last few years my daughter has only troubles from him.

Our daughter has two children who are six and ten years old. She has a lovely home and is a good housewife, but these last years it came to a point where she had to go out to work because her husband started to gamble and lost a lot of money. Because of his gambling he neglects his job. The first years after their marriage my daughter's husband was very devoted to her and to their children. But now he spends most of his time with the gamblers, and is seldom at home in the evenings.

My daughter works hard; I help her with the children, but how long can this go on? She is very depressed and suffers a great deal because her husband has changed so. She doesn't quarrel with him and even helps him out from her earnings when he has a debt to pay. She hopes that he will someday become a *mensch* again. She comes to us often with the children and pours out her bitter heart. She has never once said that she wants to leave him. It seems she still loves him.

My husband, I, and her older sisters think that she should leave him, and my question is—should we try to talk her into asking for a separation? We don't see any chance of our daughter's situation changing for the better.

We want to hear your opinion and I thank you for your answer.

Respectfully,
Mrs. N. R.

Answer:

There is really nothing to envy in your daughter's situation. To try to lead a family life with a man who has become involved with gambling is like living with a drunkard who will sell everything he owns and take milk away from his children to be able to support his bad habit.

It seems your son-in-law has a weak character and has become involved with bad friends. We wonder why your daughter doesn't try to do something about it. Isn't it possible for her to convince her husband, who she says loves her and the children, to give up these bad friends and his gambling?

It is possible that your daughter is partly to blame that your son-in-law takes everything so lightly and gambles away whatever he earns. Maybe she forgives too much and has spoiled him with her love and goodness. If this is so, she is making a big mistake. Another woman in her situation would be more firm and would insist that he take care of his obligations to his family.

There should be no talk now about a separation. Your daughter should, however, be stern with her husband and demand that he give up his gambling. If she cannot make him change, she should look for help from an agency that deals with family problems.

Worthy Editor:

I am the mother of two sons and a daughter. The sons have long since married and have given me dear grand-children, but my daughter is still with me. She has been going out with a young man over a year, but I don't know where they stand.

I have been a widow for five years and am in my sixties. I have, thank God, enough to live on, since my dear husband left me well provided for. I am close to my children and they are very dear to me, but I am unhappy because my daughter is not married yet. She is my youngest and it's good that she is at home with me, but it is high time she was married, since she's already thirty-three. My daughter is attractive, bright, and has a good office job. She had many opportunities to marry, but she was very choosy.

Lately she goes out only with this young man, but there's no talk of marriage yet. I talk to her and ask her what they are waiting for, but I get no clear answer. Since her friend comes to the house quite often, I want to ask him how long two people, who are both in their thirties, have to go together be-fore they decide whether or not they are suited to each other. But my daughter warns me not to mix in.

The young man is in business with his father and, as I understand, his family is well off. I'm waiting for my daughter to announce that they have decided to get married, but time goes on and they don't come to a decision.

My daughter is very close to me, we get along well, but as soon as I start to talk about marriage, she gets angry. I've spoken to my sons, but they tell me I must not meddle. I don't know what to do, and I beg you to advise me how to handle this problem.

With thanks and anticipation,
Mrs. F. J.

*   *   *

Answer:

We agree with you. Your daughter, already in her thirties, has been dating her friend long enough, and it's time they came to a decision.

Your daughter should not be angry with you. When you talk to her on this subject, she should realize that it's natural for you to be interested in seeing her married. It would also be quite practical for her to discuss this with her friend. It would not be wrong for them to become officially engaged at this time, if they have a reason for delaying their marriage.

But you must not be too critical of your daughter. We feel it won't be much longer until she will come to tell you the news that you have to get ready for a wedding.

Esteemed Editor:

Something recently happened to me from which I cannot seem to recover. I don't sleep nights and have to take pills to calm my nerves.

It happened a few weeks ago. I was walking home from an auxiliary meeting at three in the afternoon with several women. My friend was walking next to me, and we were talking about the business matters discussed at the meeting.

Two other friends were a few steps ahead of us, and suddenly a hooligan ran up to them and tried to take one woman's purse from her arm. She held on to it and wouldn't let go. When I saw what was happening, I started to scream "Police!" but he threw the woman to the ground, grabbed her purse, and ran. Luckily she wasn't badly hurt, and she had had only a few dollars in her purse. We helped her up, someone brought some water, and we washed the blood from her hand. Since there was no policeman around, we took a taxi and drove to the police station, where we reported the incident. Then we took the woman to her house.

I came home very upset and told my husband what had happened. Now I want to ask you: Why are these criminals and murderers allowed to roam the streets? Will our New York really continue to be a city of lawlessness? When one of these hoodlums is finally caught, he receives a light sentence and is then free to go out on the streets to his "noble profession" of robbery and murder. I think it is about time that these criminals should be punished severely.

When I talk to my husband about this he listens, agrees with me, sighs, and this is his way of calming me. He tells me things will get better in time. I see, however, that conditions are getting worse.

I hope you will print my letter and also answer me.

With respect and thanks,
Mrs. Ana R.

Answer:

The attack on a woman in midafternoon that you write about is, sad to say, no longer news because there are many such incidents occurring every day. We are living in difficult times, and it is certainly important to find ways to put an end to these robberies and murders. It is an exaggeration to say that nothing is being done about these criminals. But not enough is being done.

It is a problem that is difficult to solve. No matter how many solutions are presented, we are still vulnerable to attacks by muggers, thieves, and murderers, not only on the streets but in the subways, in the stores, and in our homes.

There has been a great deal said and written about making stricter laws and giving harsher sentences, but no one seems to know how to set this up. Let us hope that in the near future a solution to this problem will be found.

Worthy Editor:

I am writing to you about something that is going on in our family, and I will explain to you briefly what it is about.

My husband and I have been married for forty years, and we have already married off our four children. We have two sons and two daughters, who have fine families and live quite well. About six years ago my husband took one son-in-law in as a partner in his business. At that time my husband was not well, and since the business earned enough for two families, he was pleased that our son-in-law was willing to become a partner for a one-third share.

Our son-in-law proved very capable, and though he did not invest any money in the store, he has been an equal partner for some time and draws half of the profits. But lately our son-in-law has begun to take advantage. Our daughter, may she be healthy, likes to live it up. They have their own home and two dear children. Every now and then they trade in the old car for a new one; they go on long vacations, and their expenses grow with every day.

We save money from the business, but for our daughter and son-in-law it's not enough. They are always in debt. The point is that our business does not bring in any more now than it did when the expenses were not so high. So our son-in-law got the idea that we must find a way to enlarge the business. He has all sorts of plans to modernize the store, but that has to cost a great deal of money.

My husband is not interested. He doesn't have the initiative our son-in-law has. He is against the changes and feels things should go on the same way until he retires. His argument is that no matter what's done, the store won't bring in greater profits.

Lately there have been heated arguments between my husband and our son-in-law. They no longer get along, and our son-in-law has let us know he's no longer interested in staying in the business because he could get a job that would pay better. Even my daughter complains to her father, and I seem to be between two fires. I tell my husband he should give in a little. I talk to my daughter and son-in-law and tell them they don't have to conquer the world. But I get nowhere.

What is your advice? I hope you will answer my letter, and I thank you very much.

Respectfully,
Mrs. D. L.

Answer:

When your husband took your son-in-law in as his partner and saw that he worked out well, he should have foreseen that he would want to make certain changes. For your husband it may well be sufficient that everything be carried on in the old way. But a young man who is energetic and has plans for the future wants to grow with the times. He has the ambition to work his way up.

It may be that your husband is reluctant to make changes because he doesn't really believe that it's possible to pump new life into the old store. He may feel the neighborhood is not suitable. It is difficult for us to judge in this situation as to who is right, because we do not know all the facts.

But no matter what, your husband must realize that your son-in-law cannot stay on in the business if he has no chance for promotion. Therefore it would be advisable to compromise and allow your son-in-law to try his wings. But if your husband is sure that the store cannot be improved, he should try to help his son-in-law to find another position where he can advance.

Dear Editor:

More than once I've heard people say that these days you don't need a matchmaker when you have children to marry off. They consider this a custom of the past. But as far as I know, there are still enough matchmakers around who make a good living. I write this from my own experience, because I was a matchmaker once myself. I introduced my brother-in-law's son to my friend's daughter, and it became a match. Since my "profession" is to be a housewife, I didn't take any money for arranging this match.

Recently we had a lavish wedding in our family that was arranged through a matchmaker. I will tell you how this came to pass. In our family we had a girl who had all the good qualities—she was pretty, intelligent, and had a good education. But she was very shy and she couldn't seem to mix with young men. When she was in her late twenties and her mother realized that there didn't seem to be a chance of her getting married, she was distressed. The family had money, the girl earned a good salary, but there was no groom.

In time I decided to take a hand in this matter, and without asking anyone's permission, I contacted a well-known matchmaker who had a large office and asked him to arrange a match. This wasn't easy for him, because the girl's father refused to talk to him about it. The matchmaker wasn't put off, however, and in devious ways arranged a meeting between the girl and a fine young man who, like her, was shy but also very intelligent. It didn't take long and the match was arranged. The couple was married and are living happily together. I want to prove by this that matchmakers are still necessary. I thank you in advance for printing my letter.

With respect,
Mrs. N. L.

Answer:

It is true that in the course of years customs in Jewish life have changed, and today people rely on the god of love to make a match. But enough marriages are still arranged by matchmakers, who make a good living and do things in a modern fashion.

Marrying for love has become the fashion today, and the

sons or daughters of today choose their own mates. A great many young people don't want to have their parents give them any advice these days. Many of these young people feel that going to a matchmaker to arrange a match is going back to ancient times—but nevertheless there are enough marriages that are still arranged by matchmakers.

Dear Editor:

I happened to read two letters from elderly people, and, with your permission, I'd like to express my opinion.

In one letter a man over eighty complains about his children. He had hoped that the children would take their old mother and father in to live with them, but instead they put them in an old age home. The second letter is also from a man in his eighties, who lost his wife a few years ago. His children wanted him to come live with them, but he answered that he was still capable of taking care of his home and wanted to stay there.

I did it differently. I am in my late eighties and my wife is a few years younger than I. We had a wonderful life, lived in nice apartments, raised lovely children, and are respected by them and our relatives. When we saw that it was becoming too hard for us to keep up our home, we went into a fine Jewish home for the elderly. We discussed this with our children, and, though this decision was not a pleasant one for them, they agreed.

In short, we have been living in the home for seven months—it is a nice place in a resort area on the Atlantic Ocean—in the same area we had lived for thirty years. Though it is called an "old age home," which frightens many elderly people, we spend the time with nice, friendly people, our children and relatives visit us often, and we have a pleasant life there.

A friend of ours who came to visit us asked what had made us go into a home for the elderly. You are not sick, you had your children and relatives near you, this friend said. My answer was that when a couple passes the eighties and are fairly healthy, even though they have wonderful children, it is important for them to go into a good home early. It is not necessary to wait until one is helpless and make the children suffer. I hope other old people will agree with me.

With thanks and respect,
I. B.

Answer:

You did a practical thing by going into a good old age home with your wife. Old people have different ideas: Many of them refuse to stay with their children when they get old. They want to stay on in their homes and be independent as long as possible. Some of them don't want to be a burden to their children. And there are some old people who are observant and don't want to stay with their children who do not keep a kosher kitchen. There is also a question of where the children live. A large number of these children live in non-Jewish neighborhoods, and their old parents would feel very lonely there. That is why many old people do what you did.

There are, however, many older men and women who do not wish to go to an old age home, but they have no alternative. Conditions are such that there is no other way. Many of them are not happy there and complain about their children. And we also receive letters from elderly mothers and fathers who live with their children and are very happy. Their sons and daughters, sons-in-law and daughters-in-law are devoted to them and do everything possible to give them a good old age.

Dear Editor:

My wife and I have been in America some twenty-odd years and we are quite well adjusted. We keep a Jewish home, and our two sons have received a Jewish upbringing. I can't say that I am one of the most pious Jews, but I belong to an Orthodox synagogue which reminds me of a synagogue where my father worshiped in the old country. I have belonged to this congregation for many years, and here I meet familiar people. If I only had more time, I would go there more often.

My wife keeps a kosher kitchen, and she goes with me to services on Rosh Hashonah and Yom Kippur. But lately she started to tell me that we should go to the temple where her American relatives worship. She has attended several *bar mitzvahs* there, and likes their custom of seating men and women together. Since my wife has relatives and friends who belong to the temple, she wants to act more Americanized, and when it gets close to the High Holidays she starts all over again to nag me about why I drag her to the old dilapidated *shul,* where men do not sit with their wives and the services are old-fashioned. She doesn't want to understand that it is just these old-fashioned ways of my old home, which was ruined by the German murderers, that are near and dear to me.

I get along very well with my wife, but now, before the holidays, when she started all over again to insist that we go to the temple for services, I told her once and for all that she could have her way in anything but this. I told her I will not leave my synagogue. Now she is angry and insists that she's right. I would like to hear your opinion, and I ask you to answer my letter. Thank you very much.

Respectfully,
M. B.

Answer:

Your wife, who has become somewhat Americanized, has absolutely no right to give you orders as to what kind of syn-

agogue you should belong to and worship at. She may well be drawn toward the temple where her American relatives and friends belong, but she must understand that in this case her husband should have the final say. As long as she has known all this time how you love the Orthodox synagogue, which reminds you of your old homeland, she must not insist that you accede to her demands.

We live in a country where everyone has the right to live as he wishes. Surely your wife knows this; therefore it is an injustice on her part if she wants to force you to go to a temple which is not of your choice. We would like to hope that your wife will finally realize she is wrong, and will cease her blustering and raging.

Esteemed Editor:

I want to please my wife and am writing to you about something we disagree on. It will be most interesting for us to hear your opinion.

We have been married for thirty-five years and have two sons and a daughter. Our sons are married and our daughter is about to be married. I am far from wealthy, but I always made enough to keep my family in comfort and gave my children every opportunity to study. Our daughter is twenty-two years old and works in an office. She is pretty and intelligent and had many chances to marry when she was twenty, but she was very choosy. My wife was eager to see her married, but she took her time.

A year ago our daughter came home with a young man from a wealthy family, and my wife tried to talk our daughter into marrying him, but he didn't appeal to her. Six months later she met another young man who was her age, who still had a year to finish college, and she fell in love with him. He works a little and takes care of himself because he has no father, and his mother, who was widowed at forty, barely makes enough to support herself.

The boy is a fine person, and we like him very much. We thought they would wait to get married until he finished college, but after going together a few months, they came and told us they were engaged. He bought her a very nice pin as a gift and explained that he was not able to buy her an engagement ring at this time.

My wife came up with the idea that we should give them the money to buy a ring, but my daughter wouldn't hear of it. She says that a diamond ring doesn't mean anything to her—she treasures her fiancé more than any diamond. I agree with my daughter, but my wife insists that they have to buy a ring. What do you think? Thank you for your answer.

With respect,
S. M.

Answer:

We agree with your lovely, intelligent daughter who says that a diamond ring is not important. The main thing is that she is engaged to such a fine young man and that they love each other. This is worth more than diamonds or jewels.

Your wife shouldn't insist that your daughter and future son-in-law take money from you for a ring. We are sure that your future son-in-law will soon be in a position to buy your daughter many gifts, as well as a diamond ring. Keep the money and give it to them as a wedding gift to help them get settled in their new home.

Dear Editor:

I never thought that I would have to bring such a serious accusation against my husband, especially since we are now both in our fifties and have married off our two children.

The past few years I haven't been well, but my husband keeps himself looking young, and lately he has a desire to live and enjoy life. This has happened because he doesn't have to work too hard now, and our financial condition is such that we don't have to watch every dollar. We always got along well together and had a good home life. I always trusted my husband and never asked where he went or what he did. The truth is that he was always with me, and I was sure that he was true to me.

Lately he began to dress up and allow himself every pleasure. I tried to go along with him as much as I could. I never said anything to him when he went out with friends without me. More than once I convinced him to go without me.

Something happened, however, which has distressed me. I found out that my husband is having an affair with a woman who works in the same place as he. She is a Christian woman in her thirties, and he spends a lot of time in her home. It was hard for me to believe this, but when I confronted him about it he admitted it was true. He told me he had had an affair with the woman but that he had broken up with her. He begged me not to say anything about this to our children and swore that from now on, things would be different.

I have no words to express how great my resentment is, but I don't want it to become an open scandal and I don't want to upset our children. I am living with him as before under one roof, but I don't even want to talk to him.

What shall I do? I ask you for advice.

With thanks and respect,
The Betrayed Wife

Answer:

It is obvious that you had too much faith in your husband, who betrayed your trust and disappointed you so deeply. We don't know any details of his affair, but it is clear that he commited a grievous sin against you.

It is not easy for a woman to forgive and forget such ugly behavior of a husband to whom she has been married so *many years. There is no forgiving such a betrayal, and your husband should not expect you to forgive him right away.*

Since you don't want this to become public knowledge and you don't want your children to hear about it, it is advisable that you continue living under the same roof with your husband. At present there should be no thought of forgiving him, but you should not consider a separation at this time. You should make no decision until you have taken some time to calm down and think things through.

Dear Editor:

Who else but you would have the patience to listen to the troubles of people who write to you about their problems? We are also in such a situation and need your advice.

This is the second marriage for both my husband and me. During the Hitler years we both lost all our loved ones, and after being liberated, before we left Germany, we married for the second time. We planned to go to Israel to start a new life, but fate brought us to America.

I gave birth to two dear boys here, and we both worked very hard—sent our boys to a Jewish day school, then a ye-shiva, and the years passed. Our older son married a fine girl after he finished college, and he has given us a lot of joy. Our younger son, however, announced one day before he finished high school, that he was not going to go to the Orthodox day school any longer. We tried talking to him calmly and then angrily, but he wouldn't change his mind. We talked to him about going to college, but he said "no." So we didn't argue with him, and he didn't go to college. I told him that he could go to work for his father and in time could take over the business. His answer was, "I'll go away from home and you'll never see me again." I thought he was joking and said I didn't like that kind of joke. The next week, at age eighteen, he left home without a word and we didn't know where he disappeared. Don't ask what went on in our home! But we tried to get hold of ourselves. We traveled to Israel and prayed at the holy places in hopes that we would find our son.

In time we found out (through our older son) where our younger son was and sent him money so he could come home. It took a year before he returned. He began to work but he didn't live with us. Since he didn't earn enough, he came to us a year later to suggest that we take him into the business. My husband had a long talk with him, and it was decided that he should start to work and that he would take over the business when my husband retired. He is working, is very capable, and everything is fine.

Some time later, when I had to call my son late at night, a girl answered. This I didn't like. I began to ask questions and discovered that he has been living with a Christian girl for five years, and because of her, he left home. We tried everything to get him to leave her, but he loves her and won't listen to us.

Time is passing quickly, we are getting older, and we question what is to be done. I told my husband that we should speak to the girl, ask her to convert to Judaism, and have them get married. My husband doesn't want to have anything to do with either of them. What kind of advice can you give us?

With heartfelt thanks,
The Unfortunate Mother and Father

Answer:

It is not unusual for us to receive letters similar to yours, because the number of mixed marriages is increasing. Many Jewish families face the same problem. Since your son has been living with his non-Jewish girlfriend for five years, we have the feeling that you will not be able to separate them.

If you read the "Bintel Brief" column, you must be aware of the fact that we do not give definite opinions on private family matters. We do take the liberty of saying that if you want to talk to your son's girlfriend about converting to Judaism, your husband shouldn't have any objections.

Worthy Editor:

I have been in this country over twenty years and have been married sixteen years. We have a fourteen-year-old daughter whom we love dearly. I have a good job and earn a decent salary.

I married a European girl who was in the country only a year when I met her. I could have married an American girl, but I was drawn to a girl from the old country, because I had been told that American girls were spenders and bossed their husbands. I have more faith in a European girl. I cannot say that I have been unlucky, or that my wife disappointed me. She is a good housewife, does a good job raising our daughter, and doesn't neglect me.

In the beginning she was very modest and saw to it that we saved a dollar. The trouble is that she has become Americanized, and no matter how much money I give her, it is not enough. She has begun to go to the beauty parlor often, and she always finds something to buy when she goes shopping in the department stores with her friend.

She has not let me save any money for a rainy day in these last few years. As much as I earn, she squanders. I always got along well with my wife, but lately we've begun to have arguments about the money question. I am not stingy, but I like to live within my means, and my wife had changed radically in this regard. I tell her that her way of living now is not good, but my words have no effect on her. She has become a full-fledged American, as they say, and wants to live big and squanders a lot of money.

I don't want to have any arguments with my wife and I

wonder what to do. There has to be a change. I had plans to go into business for myself, but money is needed for that. My wife doesn't want to know anything about this, however. Maybe you can give me some advice about how to handle this. I will be very grateful.

Respectfully,
A Reader from New Jersey

Answer:

Your letter is not explicit. You don't say how much you earn or how much your wife spends, but we understand that your complaints about her are not unfounded. It may be, however, that you exaggerate a bit when you label her a spendthrift. You must take into account that today's inflation has raised the prices on everything.

Since you always got along well with your wife and you say that she is a good housekeeper, you shouldn't get into arguments with her. You must both have a serious talk and decide how much money you will give her each week and how much you will put into the bank. If you don't earn enough, it might be a good idea for your wife to get a part-time job.

You must make a change in your way of life. It is important that you come to an understanding and work out a budget and decide how much you need and can spend. Neither of you should allow the money problem to disturb the peace in your home.

Dear Editor:

Since you helped a dear friend of ours with your advice, I, too, turn to you with our problem and I hope you will answer soon. It's about my husband's father, that is, my father-in-law.

My husband and I are middle-aged, and our two children are already married. We are not wealthy people but my husband owns a business that brings in enough to live on decently, and we lead a fine family life. Lately, however, a problem was created by my husband's father who, until a short time ago, was also in business in a neighborhood quite a distance away from us. When he turned sixty-five he and his wife decided it was time to retire. My father-in-law and mother-in-law have two daughters, who also talked him into giving up the business. They knew that he was well-off and didn't have to work any longer. He sold the business, and for six months he and his wife had a good time. They traveled, were in Israel for several weeks, and took it easy.

In time my father-in-law got tired of his idleness and began to come in to my husband's store. He told him that he had made a mistake in giving up his business, and he wanted my husband to take him in as a partner. My husband sympathizes with his father, but he neither can nor wants to have a partner in the store. He always avoided having partners, and besides, his father had been in another line. He explains this to his father, but his sisters, who talked their father into retiring, are urging their brother to take him in as a partner.

Understandably, I, too, am against my husband making his father a partner, because I know it wouldn't work out. Now my sisters-in-law are angry with me because they think it's my fault that my father-in-law goes around dissatisfied. I am writing this letter to you with my husband's approval, and we ask you to give us your opinion on how to handle this problem. Thank you.

Respectfully,
Mrs. E. B.

Answer:

Neither you nor your two sisters-in-law should interfere in this matter. It's all up to your husband. If he doesn't need a partner and doesn't believe in partners, the question is settled and there's no more to talk about.

If your husband's father, who was a businessman for so

many years, has now realized that he retired too soon, it would not be too difficult for him to find something to do. He's not yet an old man and if he's in good health and has all his faculties, he can find himself a partner in his own line and become a businessman again, It doesn't make sense for him to force himself on his son.

If there was a question of helping your father-in-law out financially, if you had to give him a chance to earn a few dollars, it would be different. But since he is well-off, he can take care of himself and should not try to force his son to take him in as a partner.

Dear Editor:

I am a widow close to eighty. I have been living for several years with my daughter who has a dear husband and three daughters. Two are married, and the third one is getting married soon. I get along with all of them very well, and they treat me with love and respect.

I see how differently things are done these days—how young girls choose their own mates and how the most important thing to them is love. They are young and inexperienced, and yet they make their own match without consulting their parents. Boys are perhaps more mature, but they act no differently.

I have seen a lot in my own family and in families of friends, and I must say that the old-fashioned way of doing things was better. I recently had a talk with my granddaughter, who is already a mother of two children. She is very capable and has a college degree. I know that my world is not hers, but in talking with her I told her that when I was about to be married, I relied first of all on the matchmaker. The love for my husband came after we were married, because before the wedding I hadn't spoken to him.

My granddaughter was very interested in the story of my

marriage, but she laughed because she couldn't understand how you could marry a man you didn't know. I explained to her that my parents as well as my husband and I loved each other very much and were very happy in our married life. This was something she hadn't heard of before.

The world has changed and I see that the new world has brought many good things to mankind, but many bad things also. I proved to my granddaughter that the old ways of marriage were really not so bad. Then there were not so many divorces. We raised generations of children without quarrels, without separations, and without the paying of alimony.

I want to hear your opinion about this and I ask you to answer me.

With thanks and regards,
Mrs. N. M.

Answer:

It is natural that your granddaughter should think differently than you because the ideas about love and marriage are very different now than they were years ago. In the old days marriages were arranged for young couples who had no conception of love.

It cannot be said, however, that all the marriages that were then arranged by a matchmaker were successful. True, there were fewer divorces then, but only because it was considered shameful. They suffered in silence. It is also important to note that even in those days not everyone relied on the matchmakers—some couples did fall in love and arranged their own marriages.

Worthy Editor:

I am a middle-aged woman and am married to a man who has a large family, may they be well. They get together at parties, at family gatherings, and they are a very close-knit family. Some time ago my husband and I went to Israel for a few weeks, and when we got back, we had a lot of good things to tell about the Jewish land at a party that the family made for us. We also have relatives in Israel, and we talked about the good life they lead there on a *kibbutz*. Everyone was very pleased with our report.

Not long ago we had another party for several relatives who also returned from a visit to Israel. Each one of them had something to tell about the life there. One of our relatives came out with a complaint that many Jews in Israel were not religious, and he remarked that he could not understand why these people were allowed to be so unobservant. He was resentful that the Jews didn't observe *kashruth* and rode around in their cars on the Sabbath.

Since my husband and I know this man very well, and know that neither he, his wife, or his children are religious, we exchanged glances and laughed. I, however, couldn't keep quiet about the criticism of this man who keeps his store open on Saturday, eats nonkosher meat, and rides on the Sabbath, and I told him, loud enough so everyone could hear, that it was not up to him to defend orthodoxy, because he and his family were very far from being religious.

Almost everyone agreed with me. They also felt that since he is not religious, he has no right to criticize others who are not observant. The man was insulted by my remarks and insisted that in a Jewish land orthodoxy should be observed; that in America everyone might live as he pleased, but in Israel everyone should be religious.

I want to hear your opinion about this question.

With thanks and respect,
Mrs. B. K.

Answer:

Your relative shouldn't have been insulted by your remark that one who isn't religious himself has no right to criticize Israelis who aren't observant Jews. It is true that Israel is a

Jewish country, but it is also a democracy, and you cannot force every Jew to be religious.

Your relative, while he was in Israel, certainly was aware that the official day of rest there is Saturday—all businesses are closed, and people enjoy the Sabbath day of rest, each in his own way. Some of the religious Jews have their own settlements, and the government sees to it that they have every right to live as they please and that they can bring up their children in their own way. These religious Jews have their own representatives in the Knesset (Parliament) and have their say in the government.

Your relative must be made aware of the fact that the pioneers who laid the foundation of the State of Israel were nationalist Jews, most of whom were not religious. They built the Jewish homeland with blood and sweat, and many of them lost their lives in heroic battles for the independence of the Jewish state.

Dear Editor:

I need your advice and I hope you will answer me soon.

My wife and I have been together for over sixty years and we have six wonderful children—children that all Jewish parents would wish to have. We have, God bless them, seventeen grandchildren and thirteen great-grandchildren. But our life together was not what it should have been. I worked hard all these years and saw to it that we should lead a decent life, but my wife didn't appreciate it.

My wife has belonged to several Jewish organizations for many years. She gives them money when it is necessary and I never stop her. I never go along with her to the different functions of these organizations and this never bothers her. I have belonged to a synagogue for many years, and we go our separate ways.

When we are with people everything is fine, but when we are alone there is not the closeness there should be in a marriage. My wife feels that she is doing me a favor by cooking my meals. People think we get along like two doves, and I wish it were so. She is a good housekeeper, but she has absolutely no respect for me, and more than once she even insults me.

Now the thing is this: I am now over eighty-five, and, since I'm not in the best of health, I am thinking of going into an old age home alone, without my wife. I want to leave her enough money so she won't lack for anything, and let her live her life as she pleases. Our children, however, are against this. They say that it is not right, that I'll shame them if I leave home. They talk this way because they never heard me complain about their mother. Neither I nor my wife ever told them what was going on between us.

The question is—how should I act now? Do the children have the right to keep me from going to an old age home alone? I want to hear your opinion and I thank you in advance for your answer.

With respect,
M. K.

Answer:

It seems to us that you exaggerate a bit when you complain about your wife to whom you have been married for over sixty years. We cannot believe that you really have serious complaints against your wife. You, yourself, say that she is a good housewife and that you both raised six wonderful children.

We don't know what happened between you in the blessed years in which three generations arose—six children, seventeen grandchildren and thirteen great-grandchildren.

We permit ourselves to say that you should listen to your children, who are against your separating from your wife and your large family. You dare not put them to shame.

Worthy Editor:

It is hard for me to write to you because I have to complain about our daughter. It is, however, important for me and my husband to hear your opinion.

My husband and I devoted our hearts and minds to our two children—a son and a daughter. We worked very hard and gave them every opportunity to study. They both have college degrees. Our son is a professional and is the father of two children, but they live in a town far away from us. Our daughter, who is in her twenties, still lives with us and has an important job. She gives money toward the house and also saves a bit, because she earns a good salary. She is in no hurry to get married.

Our daughter is very different from our son, who is very affectionate. He visits us from time to time with his wife and children, and we go out to visit them once in a while and we enjoy being together. Our daughter, however, looks down on us. She feels superior because she is educated and, mainly, because she was born in America. She never wants to go with us to see our relatives and friends who also came from the old country.

We often have arguments with her because no matter what we tell her, she feels she knows better. My husband has words with her very often. I know she goes out with young men, but when I ask her if it is getting serious, she becomes angry with me. Recently I mentioned that a friend of hers, who is two years younger than she, is already the mother of a child, and she became so angry she warned me she would move out of the house.

I am very worried and don't know how to deal with my daughter. Perhaps you have some advice for us?

Respectfully,
Mrs. L. W.

Answer:

It is not to be believed that your daughter should act this way toward you. An intelligent person should not behave so. Just the opposite—she should show her love and appreciation to the parents who worked so hard to give her a good education.

Maybe there is a reason that she is so belligerent and feels so superior to the "old folks." Perhaps you spoiled your daughter when she was younger. You always praised her and denigrated yourselves in her eyes. There are such parents who adore their children because they are "real" Americans and because they are more educated.

Now that your daughter is in her twenties, it is hard to change her, but that does not mean that you should let her go on treating you so badly. If you can't get her to change, maybe your son should write to her to see her personally to make her see how wrong she is.

In order to keep peace in the home, it is important that you do not argue with your daughter, that you do not talk to her about getting married. Leave it up to her.

Worthy Editor:

I begin my letter with the question; Is it really degrading for a man to help his wife with her housework? This questions has caused a serious quarrel between me and our new neighbor.

My husband and I are middle-aged, and just as I sometimes help him in his business, he helps me around the house. We don't have any arrangement, because even when I didn't help him in the business, he always saw to it that I didn't work too hard. When our children were small, he helped me bathe them and did all sorts of housework.

And now, when the children are all independent, he's still the same. I don't force him to do it, he does it willingly himself. He is not one of those men whose wives lead them by the nose. He is a proud man and respected in the organization we belong to. He is not ashamed to help me wash dishes, prepare a party for guests, and when our cleaning lady doesn't show up now and then, he helps me clean the house.

A short time ago our neighbor came over to borrow something one evening and found us both in the kitchen washing the dishes, because we had just finished eating supper. Since the neighbor feels quite familiar with my husband, he began, in jest, to make fun of him because he was wiping the plates. He called him "henpecked," then, seriously, he expressed his opinion that a woman should not allow her husband to do the work of a housewife, because it degrades him. My husband smiled and simply told him it was his pleasure to spend time with his wife in the kitchen and to help her with everything. My husband even boasted that he gladly carried the clothes down to the basement washing machine because the bundle was sometimes too heavy for his wife.

But the neighbor argued his point, that a man should not do this. This made me angry, and I told him that only a narrow-minded man would make a big deal over it. I let him know that decent men are not ashamed to help their wives. I would like to hear your opinion on this question, and I thank you in advance for your answer.

Respectfully,
Mrs. F. R.

Answer:
There is a tradition from long ago that men have the duty of providing a living, while women must bear the children,

bring them up, and take care of the home. Many men and women still cling to that tradition. There are many men who will not put a hand in cold water when they are at home. No matter how hard their wives work, they feel it's beneath their dignity to help them. And there are also many women who are opposed to their husband's helping with the housework.

A great many men, who fill important positions, do not believe this. They pay no attention to these trifles, and it doesn't occur to them to feel degraded when they help their wives. Yes, there are many like your husband who, with their faithfulness and love toward their wives and children, are always ready to help out. They are not ashamed of serving their wives. They make an effort to respect and honor their wives and earn love and respect in return.

Respected Editor:

I am a woman in my fifties and am a grandmother with two grandchildren. In order to tell you what happened in my family, I must go back to the time when I was a small child. My father left home and went to America. Four years later he sent for my mother, me, and my little brother. I remember the boat trip very well, and in my childish imagination I pictured us going to a wealthy father.

However, things turned out very differently. My father worked but he made little money and we didn't have enough to eat. My mother was miserable because, in addition to the poverty, my father quarreled with her constantly. In time, I began to realize that my father was an egotist, that he brought home little money because he spent more on himself than he did on his family. He was seldom home in the evenings and lost a lot of money playing cards. My mother finally had to go out to work because she couldn't depend on my father. We had a bitter life, and it became more bitter when my mother found out that my father was having an affair with another woman. Then he abandoned us and disappeared.

After a time my mother got a divorce. She didn't want to marry again and devoted herself to my brother and me. We heard that my father had remarried and was living in the West. He didn't bother about us, and we didn't miss him. My brother and I grew up, got married, and took care of our mother. We made certain that, at least in her later years, she should have peace and pleasure. She enjoyed being with us and had a lot of joy from her grandchildren. Her last years were good ones, and three years ago she passed away.

All these years we didn't hear from my father, but suddenly my brother received a letter from him saying that he was old and sick, that his wife had died a long time ago, and that he was in a hospital not far from New York. He had found my brother's address and wanted to see us before he died. He wrote that he knows he doesn't deserve to have us come to visit him.

My brother went to see him, and when he got to the hospital he had to ask someone to take him to his father. They brought him to a bed upon which lay an old man who was only skin and bones. My father didn't say much but told my brother that he wishes to see me too. It is hard for me to go to him because I can't forget how he treated our mother.

I want your opinion.

With thanks and respect,
Mrs. E. T.

Answer:

Your father doesn't really deserve to have you visit him and it is understandable that you have no desire to see him. How can you have any feelings for a father who abandoned his children and their mother?

We can't persuade you to visit your father and show him any love, but he is, after all, your father and you don't have to repay him in the same coin. We believe that if your mother were alive, she would want you to see your father. If you decide to visit your father, we suggest that you do not bring up the past and berate him for his behavior.

Worthy Editor:

My wife and I have been together for over forty years and never had any real quarrels. We have two fine children, who now have their own families, and we always lived respectably and honorably. I am in business and made a fine living for my family. I never begrudged my wife anything, and she never lacked for money. I always had the fullest trust and confidence in my wife.

Not long ago, however, one evening when I was already in bed and supposedly asleep, I saw my wife take a few dollars from my pocket. If I hadn't seen it, I wouldn't have known that she had taken any money, because when I come home from the store at night I am tired and never count the day's earnings that I bring home.

Next morning I didn't ask her what she was looking for in my pockets because I thought she would tell me herself. I didn't say anything but I kept an eye on her and saw that in the evenings, when I was supposed to be asleep, she went to my pocket and took out two or three dollars, and sometimes even more.

A few weeks later, I finally had my say. As a rule I leave my wife money for the week every Thursday morning before I go to the store. On Thursdays she goes food shopping for the Sabbath and the rest of the week. This Thursday I didn't leave her any money. When she called me later to tell me I had forgotten to leave her money, I calmly told her that I didn't forget but that she should use the money she stole from my pockets.

These words started an avalanche. She started to quarrel with me and complained about me to the children. She claims that it never occurred to her that I would consider it "stealing" when she took a few dollars out of my pocket. She is angry that I spied on her, and she feels that she is in the right. Therefore, I want to hear what you think about this.

With respect,

A. B.

Answer:

In order to make a judgment in this case, we would have to hear what the other party has to say. We take the liberty, however, of saying to both of you that first, your wife should not have taken money from your pockets without telling you, second, that you were wrong in not asking her immediately what she was looking for in your pockets, and third, that you should both do everything possible to see to it that this does not lead to a quarrel that will make your lives miserable.

Worthy Editor:

I am very disturbed about my husband to whom I have been married for forty years, because his behavior is very different from what it used to be. We never had any arguments about money, but now it seems because of the inflation, which gets worse each day, we are constantly arguing.

Our children are all married, and there are just the two of us at home. The children and grandchildren come to visit us often, and of course it is my greatest pleasure to prepare foods for them that they like, and for this I need a little more money.

I know that my husband, who is not so young, doesn't earn much, but because of inflation he has received several raises in salary. However he doesn't want to touch the money he has received in raises. I don't say we should stop saving. In fact, I often remind him that we should put away some money for our old age. My husband has always been a kind man, devoted to the children, but lately he gives me a hard time when I go shopping for food. When it is time to eat, however, he likes to see the best of everything on the table.

Since I want to avoid quarrels, I have suggested that he do the food shopping. I want him to see how the prices for food have risen so that he will realize that I don't ask for more money than I need. But this he doesn't want to do either.

He doesn't understand that I also need to buy some things for myself once in a while. If the children didn't bring me gifts—a dress or a blouse—I wouldn't have anything to wear. It will reach the point where I will probably have to get myself a job. What can be done? Please give me some advice.

With respect,
Mrs. S. K.

Answer:

Women are not always justified in their complaints that their husbands do not give them enough money to run the house. Just as there are men who are careful with a dollar, there are women who never have enough, no matter how much money they are given.

In your case, however, it seems to be different. Your husband doesn't want to realize that the raises he is getting in his salary are to cover the rise in the cost of living. This means that these monies are not to be put in the bank, but are to be put in the stomach. They are to be used for food, clothing, and other necessities.

You should get your children to explain this to your husband

Dear Editor:

I have been suffering a long time because my wife's addiction to playing Bingo has become an obsession, and I cannot stand it any longer.

My wife is by nature quiet and calm, but she has gotten involved with Bingo and goes out to play three and four evenings a week. Since she is afraid to go out alone at night, she drags me along and I have to go. I have no patience for it, and I sit there like a zombie.

The Bingo playing is also expensive. No matter how you play, it costs money and time. I had a talk with my wife and showed her that she was wasting money and time on this devilish game, but her answer was that I should be happy that she plays only three or four nights a week, not like other women who play every day and spend a lot of money. She feels she is saving me money, and I don't appreciate it. Other women, she adds, smoke two packs of cigarettes while playing and eat and drink there, which costs a lot, and she doesn't do this.

When I sit there, I see that, in comparison with the other women, my wife is really more restrained, but even her restraint costs me money, and it becomes more and more of a burden for me. I keep telling her that the game is a delusion—that no one can win—but my talk is in vain. I cannot understand why the government allows this Bingo playing. Poor people lose the money they need to buy food and clothing at this game.

What's to be done? Where does one find a solution? How does one tear a woman away from the Bingo obsession? I hope you will print my letter and give me some advice as to what to do.

I thank you in advance,
W. M. A.

Answer:

Unfortunately, there are no special cures for the "illness" of Bingo, cards, or other like games, which were created for enjoyment and relaxation, but which some people have turned into gambling games.

You complain that the government doesn't ban Bingo, but you forget that this is really no more than a game for pleasure, as compared with other gambling like betting on the horses, numbers, etc. Gambling in America and other countries has become big business, and although it is clear that it does a lot of damage and demoralizes many people, nothing is done to stop it.

You should be able to solve your problem by yourself. You should not have allowed your wife to go out several nights a week to play Bingo. You should have tried to find other ways for her to find enjoyment and certainly, you should not give in to your wife and go along with her to the Bingo games. Another person cannot help you in this instance. You must try to convince your wife to give up playing Bingo. This may mean, however, that you have to take her to other places where she will find enjoyment and relaxation.

Dear Editor:

Several times I have read in your paper about mixed marriages and each time I am reminded of our own experience because the same thing happened to us.

We have two children, a son and a daughter. We gave them a Jewish upbringing and we always observed Jewish tradition in our home. We are not Orthodox (my husband keeps the store open on Saturday), but I always kept a kosher kitchen and we go to synagogue on Rosh Hashonhah and Yom Kippur. Our son has a fine Jewish wife, and they lead a life like ours. Our daughter, who is seven years younger than our son, fell in love with a Christian boy while she was in college, and we didn't know anything about it for a while.

Once when she made a party at home she also invited her Christian friend. Although my husband and I spent the whole evening in another room in order not to interfere with the young people, I noticed the blond young boy and realized that he was not Jewish. I also felt that my daughter was very interested in him. That night I didn't sleep, and the next morning I had a talk with my daughter. But neither my talking nor my husband's had any effect. Her answer was that she loved him. We couldn't tear her away from this young man, who is a professional, and in time they were married. They moved far away from us, and we didn't see them for a year. I missed my daughter very much, and then one day she came to see us unexpectedly to tell us she was expecting a child in a few months, that her husband was going to convert to Judaism, and that they wanted a Jewish name for their child.

In short, our son-in-law became a Jew. Our daughter gave birth to a daughter, and the child was given a Jewish name in the synagogue. I want to say that it is not a question of asking someone else for advice as how to act in these matters. One has to act as the heart dictates.

With respect,
Mrs. B. R.

Answer:
These days it is not news when children bring home non-Jewish sons- or daughters-in-law to their parents. To our regret, the number of mixed marriages is increasing. Jewish parents, even those who are not religious, do not approve of mixed marriages, but enough parents make peace with it in time because their love for their children is stronger than anything else.

The fact that your son-in-law converted must make you very happy, and you were right not to get angry and to keep a close relationship with the couple. Your comment that one *cannot ask advice from others in a matter of this sort is correct. It is a private family matter, and each one must handle it according to his feelings and principles.*

Worthy Editor:

My first wife thought very highly of the "Bintel Brief," and more than once we read together your wise answers to those who wrote to you. Therefore I decided to appeal to you about something that is going on between me and my daughter.

My wife and I raised three children, a daughter and two sons, who are now all married. We were always close to our children, but a short time ago my daughter, who is the oldest, became angry with me, and I am very troubled.

I lost my wife, with whom I had lived for forty happy years. She was sick for almost a year, and I did everything to save her. But the doctors could not help her. I was left alone in my home, and it was a bitter time for me. The children live quite a distance away and couldn't help me, since they are busy with their families. From time to time I visited them, and at times they came to me and they could see how lonely I was. My sons were the first to tell me I should marry again. And in time, when I met an old friend of ours, a widow, I began to think I should listen to them.

Last winter, the woman whom I was beginning to see often was planning to go to Florida, and she talked me into going too. So, nine months after my wife's death, we got married and left for Florida. It's over a year now that I've been married to my second wife, and we are content because we both have had a taste of being alone. But my daughter got angry with me because I married so soon. My sons understand quite well the position I was in and they don't scold me for my haste in marrying, but my daughter thinks I shouldn't have married at all. I'm sure that if she were to come to my home and see that I'm living like a human being again, she would be happy. But she is angry with me and doesn't want to come. I am troubled about this because I always got along well with my children, and I don't know what to do about it.

I want to hear your opinion and advice, and I thank you in advance for your answer.

Your reader,
L. F.

Answer:

Many men and women who were happy in their first marriages marry again when they remain alone. Their children, who are by that time independent, should not interpret this as wrong, and should not resent it. We mean to say that your daughter should not think that you have erased the memory of her deceased mother by marrying a second time.

It may be that your daughter does not realize how hard it was for you to live alone when you lost your wife. She should take the example set by her brothers, who did realize that it was quite practical for you to marry again.

Worthy Editor:

Many years ago I wrote to you for advice, and I still remember your sensible answer that helped me a great deal. Now I am writing to you about a relative's problem, and I hope that you will be able to help her also.

My cousin has been married for twelve years and has three children. The youngest is a boy of four, and he is left-handed. My cousin doesn't consider this a fault and doesn't pay any attention to it. But her husband is different. He says that a normal person does everything with his right hand and insists that the boy shouldn't use his left hand. My wife cannot stand to see how he tortures the child. I myself was once there and saw him give his son a slap when he started to eat with his left hand.

I once said to my cousin's husband that these days people don't make an issue of this, and that even teachers in school don't interfere when the children write with their left hands. But he gave me an angry look that said I shouldn't interfere. My cousin is an intelligent woman and knows that her husband's actions are making their child very nervous, and this leads to serious arguments between them. His attitude comes from the fact that he too was left-handed as a child and he was beaten many times until he started using his right hand. He forgets, however, that that was in the old country and many years ago. He doesn't want to realize that today in this country, being left-handed is not considered a fault.

You cannot imagine how upset my cousin is. The child has become very nervous and is losing weight. Recently she took him to a doctor, and he too said the child should not be forced to use only his right hand. But her husband doesn't want to listen to anyone. Maybe you have some advice? I thank you in advance for your answer.

With respect,
Mrs. R. L.

Answer:

It is unbelievable that your cousin's husband doesn't want to listen to anyone. We feel that he is harming his child. He should realize that it is important to leave his child in peace. His actions could lead not only to the breaking up of his home, but will also harm his child.

It is as you said—today there is no stigma attached to being left-handed. There are many left-handed people who have become famous in their various careers. In the olden days it was different. Left-handed children were made to suffer a great deal by their parents and teachers. But today people who are left-handed are not ashamed of it and are not interfered with. Your cousin should insist that her husband go with her and their child to the doctor, and perhaps he will then follow his advice.

Worthy Editor:

I am a woman in my thirties, a mother of two children, and I have a fine husband to whom I have been married fifteen years. He has a good job and takes good care of his family. Neither I nor the children have any complaints against him. Lately, however, I am annoyed about my husband's parents, who are not old people.

The thing is this: My mother-in-law and father-in-law used to live far away from us, and we didn't see them often. About a year ago they moved to our neighborhood, and we not only helped them get settled but we always invited them to our home. While their place was being fixed up, we asked them to sleep at our home.

We showed them a lot of devotion and friendship, and they always felt very comfortable in our home. But they soon began to mix into everything in our lives and spend more time in our home than in their own. They have a key to our house and don't wait for an invitation. They come and go as they please. This wouldn't bother me, but they make changes in my home. I once went away for a few hours and when I returned, I was astounded to see how they were making themselves at home there. First of all, they didn't like how the furniture was arranged and they moved it around to their liking. My mother-in-law didn't ask me, but in the evening she stood near the kitchen and announced that she was making a special treat for supper. I have hinted to her several times that our tastes are different from theirs, but it doesn't help.

My husband is very attached to them and he doesn't want them to be hurt, but we don't know what to do. My husband

had a little argument with them when they came in one evening unexpectedly. We had important guests, and though they
didn't know the people, my father-in-law got into a conversation with them, which upset the guests as well as us.

We don't want to quarrel with them, but what's to be
done? I beg you to answer me.

With thanks and respect,
Mrs. H. S.

Answer:

*From what you write about your in-laws, it is clear that
they are strong-willed, and it was not hard for them to force
their will upon you. We can imagine how upset you are when
they come to your home and start to assert themselves. The
thing is, that in a way both you and your husband are to
blame, because right from the beginning you spoiled them and
let them do whatever they wanted to.*

*Since it has gone too far, you and your husband must now
institute a new regime. This doesn't mean that you should
quarrel with your husband's parents, but both you and your
husband must talk to them openly. They must be told that
they cannot do whatever they want to in your home and that
they should not mix into your lives.*

Dear Editor:

I am now a man over fifty and because of various reasons,
I never married. I remained an old bachelor, and lately I regret
the fact that I didn't marry when I was a young man. Now it is
too late, because at my age it isn't a good idea to make a
change in my life.

As I grew older people began to avoid me because I was a
bachelor. They called me "Old Bachelor" and almost forgot

my real name. They made jokes at my expense and more than once told me I never married because I didn't want to feed a wife.

Almost a year ago I was offered a good job in another city, and I moved there. I wanted to start a new life. I settled in a Jewish neighborhood and thought that everything would now be fine. Since I had learned from experience that people didn't think much of a bachelor, I decided, in this city where no one knew me, to tell people I was a widower. At first I was very happy with this idea. However, I found I had created another problem: In the city where I used to live, people knew that the "Old Bachelor" would never marry. When the people here heard that I am a widower and that I have been alone for several years, I was besieged by matchmakers. I tell them I am not interested in getting married but it doesn't help.

If I don't have enough trouble from the matchmakers and friends who try to introduce me to women, there are widows who are always around. They don't wait for a matchmaker—they know how to trap a man themselves. It has become very uncomfortable for me, and the only solution seems to be to run away from here. I never knew there were so many widows in the world.

What shall I do? Maybe you have some advice for me.

                                With thanks and respect,
                                    S. L.

·

Answer:

We don't know what kept you from marrying when you were a young man, and it is also not clear to us why you don't get married now. It is, however, clear to us that you are far from happy.

It seems you suffer from an inferiority complex. You think that people look at you queerly because you are a bachelor. We think this is highly exaggerated. As far as we know, there are many bachelors who are accepted in the finest society, and no one cares whether they are married or not.

Worthy Editor:

I beg you to help me unravel the knots in my tangled life. The thing is that in the last ten of my seventy-five years, I have been feeling worse and worse. It began when I became a widower and then, fifteen years ago, married again. I found a nice woman, but she is sickly. If she didn't have problems with her nerves, we would get along well.

In the summer we go to the country quite often for a few days' rest, but in the past few years she has been insisting that we also go to Florida in the winter. She says she feels better when she goes away. I give in to her on most things, but my conscience has begun to bother me, and I ask why my first wife never had the luck to be able to get away and rest from her hard work. My first wife bore and raised children and also went out to work. She never demanded anything and never complained.

Thanks to our present circumstances, my second wife doesn't need to work. However, she makes demands and wants to be like all the women she knows. She may be right, but I go around with a feeling of guilt toward the mother of my children. My conscience bothers me whenever we are getting ready to go somewhere, and I think constantly about my first wife, who was always working. I also think—should I be wasting money when my children need my help?

All this is on my mind every minute. Do I have the right to enjoy life with my second wife? All these thoughts disturb my relationship with my second wife and lead to a feeling of enmity. Therefore, I seek help from you. Maybe I should go to a psychiatrist about my condition? I beg you to answer me.

With thanks and respect,
N. P

Answer:

We think that it was important for you to write this letter. The fact that you got things off your chest should have helped you.

After reading your letter, we believe you are torturing yourself needlessly. You should not have gotten yourself into the predicament of having these guilt feelings that you wronged your first wife because she could not enjoy the things you are giving your second wife.

You forget that life was different years ago than it is today. Your first wife had to help you in those years to make a living because wages were low then. Were she alive today, she could enjoy all the things your second wife does. You must realize that many changes occurred during these years, and you should see to it that you lead a peaceful life with your second wife.

Dear Editor:

I am one of those retired men who worked in a shop for many years, and since many letters are printed in the "Bintel Brief" about these people, I also want to write, with your permission, about how life is for me as a retired person.

I read about older people who have stopped working and complain that they don't know what to do with their free time. I, however, do not have this problem. When I became sixty-five my wife urged me to stop working. She pointed out that we have more than enough to live on from the money we saved, from our Social Security, and from the union pension. Our three married children, who are all doing quite well, also said it was time I should retire. Since I had my strength and mental capacity, and since I feared sitting around doing nothing, I was in no hurry to give up the shop. At sixty-seven, I decided I had worked enough and it was time for me to retire.

This was four years ago, and I can say that life was never so good for me and my wife as it is now. We are busier than ever and we have a lot of pleasure. We belong to several organizations, we visit the children, they visit us, we see friends, we spent the winter in Florida, summer in the mountains, and we know what it is to enjoy life. My wife and I are, thank goodness, in good health, and it is no exaggeration to say that in the last few years we have become younger, not older. We always had a good family life, never quarreled, and so it is now. I help my wife, go shopping with her, and want her to feel that she also has partially retired.

It all depends on how one arranges one's life. The important thing is not to let yourself go so that your wife considers you a person who doesn't amount to anything. I am writing this in the hope that my letter will give other retired people courage and they will not feel that they are useless.

With respect,
L. N.

Answer:

It is true that we have printed many letters about the problems of retirement. But it is a topic that is always timely, and we are therefore glad to print your letter. We are sure that many elderly people will be interested in reading your letter, in which you write about how good and beautiful life can be when one stops working.

There are people who believe that one should keep working as long as one can, and give up the shop only when one's strength fails. Lately, however, there are many people who cannot wait for the time that they will be able to stop working. They are healthy and strong but they want to retire as early as possible so that they can enjoy life longer.

The main trouble with many people is that for years their only interest was work. The shop or their business was their whole world, and they had no other interests. They have to be taught how to fill their free time. More and more is being done in this area. Clubs are organized in which older people can

find an interest; some are drawn into organizational work;
concerts and other entertainments are planned for them. But
the problem is far from being solved.

Worthy Editor:

My husband and I are now elderly, and the question arose
as to whether people in their declining years should leave a
legacy to children who do not deserve it. We often talk about
our children, who are long since married and who have very
little time for their parents. We have two sons and a daughter,
all of whom have grown-up children, but they are always
busy, and we live in loneliness. We are not rich, but we always
saw to it that our children wanted for nothing. Our daughter
does come to visit us once in a while, but our sons seldom
show up.

Over a year ago my husband became ill and they had to
take him to the hospital where he spent over two weeks. I
telephoned the children, but only our daughter came one time
to see him. Our sons didn't come to the hospital at all. When I
was sick and also taken to the hospital, my only visitor was
my sister, who lives not far from us. I'm glad we are close to
my sister, who is ten years younger than I, because she always
finds time to help us out.

We don't need financial aid from our children. We have
Social Security and we've also saved a little money for our
later years. We still give gifts and money to our grandchildren
when there's an occasion.

Since we're not getting younger but older, we often talk
about whether we should leave a legacy to our children. Unfortunately, they have not shown any interest in devoting any
time or thought to their old feeble parents. My husband thinks
that our two sons do not deserve to be mentioned in our will.
But I feel differently. They are, after all, our children and deep

in our hearts we love them. Therefore, we want to hear your opinion, and I beg you to answer in the "Bintel Brief."

With respect and thanks,
Mrs. T. Z.

Answer:

Your disappointment in your children is probably not unfounded, and they should be scolded for their attitude toward you. But we want to mention that sometimes the parents are guilty when the children alienate themselves. It often happens that misunderstandings occur when parents demand too much from their sons and daughters, who are involved in their own families and businesses.

But there are also heartless children who think only of themselves and don't care whether their parents live in loneliness. Since we are not acquainted with all the details, and do not know how much you possess, we have no right to state a positive opinion. But we believe that even now you must try to draw the children closer to you, and you should try to convince your husband to accept your opinion.

Dear Editor:

I write this letter to you in the name of several women who are neighbors of mine in a large apartment house. The issue is a young neighbor of ours, a woman of thirty-odd years, who has three young children. As far as we know, her husband left her, and it seems he doesn't send her enough money to live on, since the young, pretty children are very poorly dressed. The woman, who is quite attractive, doesn't go to work, but she dresses very well. We heard that she goes to a drama school and is learning to be an actress. She goes off in the morning, comes home for a while to take a peek at the children, then goes back to the school.

The children, who are from six to nine years old, are always by themselves. The two older ones are in school till afternoon, and the youngest boy remains alone. The neighbors talk among themselves about how these children are neglected. But we don't know what to do about it. Some of them tried, on occasion, to talk to the woman about the children, who wander about the streets, but she got angry and said that nobody had to worry about them.

The little boy knocks at a neighbor's door to say hello, and when he's given a glass of milk or something to eat, his eyes light up. Something should be done about this. After all, there are social agencies, and we could inquire about an institution. But we hold back, because it is quite possible that bringing this out into the open could make the situation worse. We don't want to make trouble for the mother.

Therefore, we decided to turn to you to hear what you have to say about this.

With thanks and respect,
A Group of Neighbors

Answer:

Though we know that sometimes it happens that a mother neglects her children, it is hard for us to believe that your neighbor is so heartless. Perhaps the situation is not so bad and you are exaggerating a bit.

The woman has the right to forbid you to meddle in her family life. But if it is clearly proven that she really is neglecting her children, then you may step in. It is a very delicate situation, and since we do not know what is going on with the separated couple, we cannot give you a definite answer. It would be advisable if the closest neighbor could talk to the woman in a friendly way about this when she has an opportunity.

Worthy Editor:

I wrote you many years ago to ask for help in solving an argument that came up in our women's club, and I am very thankful for your good advice.

Now I come to you about something that has to do with my husband, with whom I have been living for over forty years. We always had a good family life, brought up fine children, and even led a grandchild to the altar. We are both in our late sixties, but my problem is that my husband still wants to act like a young man. This makes me ashamed when we are with people and he dances around the young women and becomes so busy he forgets everything.

The fact that he has this weakness for women is not news to me, because he was always like this. This is his nature. He loves to be a "gentleman," and I never interfered with him because I always had complete trust in him. I was sure he didn't mean any harm. Now that we are no longer young and have grown grandchildren, I cannot stand his acting the fool around the young women. I think at this age one shouldn't make himself ridiculous, and it bothers me when I see our friends exchanging sly smiles when they see how he acts. But when I tell this to my husband, he thinks I am jealous, even though he knows it's not in my nature. When I show him that people are laughing at him, he says it's because they envy his success with women who are much younger than he. And I cannot convince him.

I must add that otherwise I have no complaints about my husband. He is very good and devoted to me and the children. The only thing is that his "weakness" is causing me a lot of grief now. I ask you to give me your opinion, because I think I am right, not my husband.

> With thanks and respect,
> Mrs. E. B.

Answer:

We agree with you that it is not right for a man in his sixties to act like a young man. We think, however, that you are taking your husband's "weakness" too seriously. It is not your nature to be jealous. You yourself say that your husband doesn't mean anything by his dancing around young women, but it seems that it does bother you a great deal. If it does bother you so much, you should both have a serious talk before it develops into a quarrel. A couple who has lived together forty years in love and devotion should not allow such a minor thing to mar the peace in their home. You should both take this into account.

You should not demand that he suddenly change. You yourself say that his character is such. Therefore you should not expect him to change all at once.

Worthy Editor:

I am writing to you about the aggravation we are having with our son, who is not getting along well with his wife.

Our son is very successful. He has a good job and earns a fine living. The trouble is that he was too particular, and he was so fussy for so long that he finally made a bad choice. Three years ago when he was already thirty he married a twenty-one-year-old girl. Our son married her soon after they met. He hardly knew her when they went to the altar. She is pretty, and he fell in love with her right away. He brought her to our home before the marriage, and she appealed to us. We were not against the match, but my husband and I could not convince them not to marry so hastily.

At first, everything was fine and dandy and they lived a good life. His wife looked up to him because she was a European immigrant. She was fifteen when she came here with her parents. She managed to study here a bit, but our son brought her into a fine society and gave her status. She paid attention and learned a great deal from her husband.

Barely a year after the marriage she gave birth to a child, and all was fine. At first she was grateful for everything, but this did not last long. She soon adjusted to life here and began to act more Americanized. She got acquainted with self-indulgent women who began to teach her to take advantage of all the good things. It went so far that she decided she wanted a maid to take care of the child and run the house while she spent her days at the beauty parlor, playing cards, or going to the big department stores to shop.

When our son realized how she had changed, he first tried talking calmly and quietly to her, but when she didn't even want to hear him out, they began to quarrel and there's no longer any peace in their home. Our son still loves his wife but he's very depressed and doesn't know what to do. Possibly you have a suggestion. I beg you to answer soon.

With thanks and hope,
Mrs. L. B.

Answer:

It is unbelievable that your daughter-in-law has changed so under the influence of her new girlfriends. According to your letter, the couple was deeply in love, and she was grateful and looked up to her good man. Maybe there are other reasons that led up to such an upheaval in their family life. Is it possible that your son is partly to blame?

We question whether you know exactly what is going on between the two of them. We also wonder what your son thinks about the changes in his wife. We cannot understand how your young daughter-in-law, who worshiped her husband, could now start quarreling with him. Does she want a separation? Has she forgotten that they have a young child?

We feel that if the situation is so serious and strained, it is important that they consult a marriage counselor, who could help them restore their former good relationship.

Honorable Editor:

I am an elderly woman, and even though I have two children and grandchildren, I am very lonely. Four years ago I lost my husband and I miss him very much. I don't complain to my children because I know they are involved with their own families. I spend time with them quite often, but this is not enough for me and most of my time I live in loneliness. My children are ready to help me with money, but I don't need it. My devoted husband left me well provided for. Of course, I'd like it very much if my sons and daughters-in-law could give me more attention, because the older I become, the more difficult it is for me to be alone.

Of late I haven't been feeling well, and it is getting harder for me to keep up my apartment. Some of my friends tell me I should give it up; others say I should take someone in to share the apartment. My neighbor kept telling me I should remarry, but I didn't want to hear about it. First of all, I knew I'd never find another man as good as the one I lost, and second, I was close to seventy when my husband died—too late to think of marrying.

My children do not have much time for me and I think it might be wise for me to give up my apartment and go into an old age home for the years I have left. Truthfully, I have no great desire to go to a home, but I don't see any alternative. I feel that I am getting weaker and I'm afraid that later on I may not be accepted into a home.

I want to hear your opinion about this. I have a nice home

with many beautiful things, and I have to decide whether to give it all up. I hope you will answer me soon.

With respect and thanks,
Mrs. H. F.

Answer:

Although you write very little about your children, we feel that you are very disappointed in them, and you are justified in your feelings. They know that their mother is old and weak, and they should make an effort to spend more time with you. It is also their duty to help you decide what is best for you. It is certainly better to be in your own home, but if it is getting to be too difficult for you and you can no longer be alone, there is nothing wrong in going into a good home for the elderly. Another solution would be to take a woman into your home to share the work. It is important that you discuss this matter with your children.

Worthy Editor:

I and my family came to America from Russia six years ago. Since I've become a reader of the *Forward* here, in which I find many interesting articles, I recently read something in the "Bintel Brief" that interested me very much. It was a letter from a man who wrote about becoming estranged from his relatives who brought him to America. He explained that in the beginning his family helped him a lot but later something happened which caused them to drift apart.

I have read other letters in the "Bintel Brief," where newcomers to the States complain about their American relatives. Therefore I ask your permission to tell them they shouldn't complain. The fact that these relatives helped them to come to America means they did a lot. Especially those who have been helped to get out of Russia should accept whatever is done for them and be grateful. They shouldn't forget what they went through in Russia.

Those who complain know full well that those who remain there with Brezhnev would be satisfied with one potato a day if they could be helped to come to America. Here one is free, and anyone who has the strength to work can make a living.

Of course, in the beginning one has problems here also. I had them too, but I cannot forget that my relatives brought me to this free land and helped me so much. I will always be thankful to them for getting me out of Russia. My family and I will always appreciate this.

I hope you will print my letter, and I thank you in advance.

With great respect,
S. L. S.

Answer:

From time to time we receive and print letters from new immigrants who complain about their American relatives. In certain cases these complaints are justified, because the relatives they find here have disappointed them. More than once the newcomers from across the sea have met relatives who have hearts of stone. These are, however, unusual cases.

After the Hitler tragedy when the survivors came to America in the thousands, the heartfelt reception and the tremendous help they received from their American relatives was a healing balm and solace for them. Most of these immigrants appreciated, as you do, what their relatives did for them, and had nothing but praise and thanks.

There were, however, and still are, among these immigrants some who found it difficult to acclimate and live with their relatives here. They were broken in spirit and they are like the sick man who cannot find a comfortable place for

*himself no matter where he is put. And when one is sick, he
pours out his bitterness to those nearest to him. But there are
very few who complain.*

Dear Editor:

This letter is being written by a widow in her seventies,
and I ask your advice about a delicate matter. The thing is
this:

Seven years have passed since I lost my husband. Since
then I have been alone taking care of myself. I have a son and
daughter, but they live far from me and I don't see them often.
I lead a lonely life, and in addition, lately I am not well. I am
beginning to feel my age. My children talk to me frequently on
the telephone and want me to come to visit them, but it is too
far for me to go for a visit. I have enough to live on, thank
goodness, and don't have to ask them for help. I even send my
grandchildren money on various occasions, and they give me
lots of joy when my children bring them to visit me.

The thing is that it is bitter to live in loneliness. A while
ago I met my husband's *landsman* in the park, and we were
both glad to have someone to talk to. He is a fine man and is
also lonely because he has been a widower for several years.
After we saw each other a few times, he asked me to marry
him. He is my age and retired a few years ago. He is not
wealthy but is assured of an income. It seems that I would
have to contribute some of my income to the household if we
were to marry.

It is possible that it would be better for both of us if we
were to get married. One of my friends who knows him very
well has nothing but praise for him. The thing is that I haven't
been well for several weeks. I've told him about it and he
assures me that I need not worry, that he will be a good friend

and will help me with the housework. I don't know what to do and it is very important for me to hear your opinion.

I ask you to answer me soon.

With respect,
Your thankful reader,
A Woman from the East Side

Answer:

We read your letter carefully, and it is not hard for us to realize how lonely life is for you since you lost your husband. Loneliness has caused many men and women to remarry.

We know little about you and even less about your friend—therefore we have no right to tell you whether to marry him or not. We feel that in this case you should discuss it with your children. It is important that you hear what they have to say. You should also get to know your friend better. We want to note that it is not news for men and women of your age to marry a second time.

Dear Editor:

I now have the need to write to you about a serious problem and I beg you to help me with your advice.

The problem deals with our son, who is a professional and has, for three years, held a position out West. There he fell in love with a gentile girl, though he had a good Jewish upbringing. She wrote to us asking us to give our permission for them to marry. We were very much against it; then she wrote again, telling us she was going to convert to Judaism and would observe the Jewish traditions, and begged us not to stand in the way of their marriage.

My husband and I took the letter to the rabbi of our congregation, and he told us to give our consent. We did so with heavy hearts, and they were married. A short time ago they came to us with their child. They have been with us for a few weeks, and I can tell you that our daughter-in-law leads a more Jewish life than we do. She blesses the candles Friday night and observes the laws of *kashruth*. We fell in love with her right away and everything is fine.

I have a mother and a father who are elderly people and very religious. They were absolutely opposed to the marriage and got mad at their grandson, even though they loved him very much. They live in a city not far from us, with a sister of mine, and now it's like this: my sister is planning a wedding for her daughter in a few weeks. We, as well as our son and daughter-in-law, are invited to the affair.

But since my parents have completely shut out our son, he wonders whether he and his wife should accept the invitation. I am trying to talk them into going to the wedding so he can introduce his wife to his grandparents. I think that when she talks to them about Judaism, they'll change their opinion of her.

We would like to hear your advice, and I thank you in advance for your answer.

Respectfully,
Mrs. R. L.

Answer:
  We feel that the wedding where the whole family will be gathered would be a good opportunity to make peace between your son and your parents, and to acquaint them with his young wife. If you are now pleased with the match, and your daughter-in-law has adjusted to you so well, then there is no reason for your parents not to accept her as part of the family.

  Your son and his wife should accept the invitation, and you must definitely see to it that your parents and the young couple come to an understanding. But it would be advisable to prepare your parents for this meeting. You must tell them about your daughter-in-law's conversion to Judaism, and that she is now part of the family.

Worthy Editor:

I am writing this letter to you in the name of several retired men. During the summer months we got together in the park and discussed the news of the world. We talked and talked until we got to the subject of the old days. Most of the men said that everything was better then. I doubt whether it really was better years ago. I believe that when an older person longs for the old days, it's because then he was young with his whole life ahead of him.

My opinion is that the good old days were not that good. I remember very well the small towns in the old country. I remember that our house was a poor hut, and in the evenings the only light we had was from a little kerosene lamp; the streets were not paved and during the rainy season the mud made it impossible to get around. The poverty was so bad there that when we came to New York and settled on the East Side, we thought it was paradise.

But fifty or sixty years ago, even here life was difficult for the newcomer. Most of the immigrants lived on the East Side in dilapidated tenements. The rooms were small and dark, there was no bathroom in the apartment, only a large tub in the kitchen near an old iron stove. Who doesn't remember the "good old days" in the sweatshops, where one worked fourteen to sixteen hours a day and the workers were treated like slaves. These days life is better for the workers and for people in general. People live comfortably and the new inventions have brought ease and plenty. The homes have all sorts of electrical appliances to make life easier, and here in this blessed land one has every opportunity to better himself.

When I said that one doesn't have to yearn for the old days, only a few agreed with me. According to them, in those years people got along better on less. They were more satisfied because they didn't have to strive so hard.

We'd like to hear your opinion.

With respect,
L. P. W.

Answer:

We agree with you that the old days that people long for cannot be compared with the present, and that your conclusion is correct. We've come a long way from the poor homes with the kerosene lamps in the old country to the modern way of life here. It is quite natural that some older people yearn for the past and see that time in a rosy light. It is as you said— they yearn for their youth, when they had their whole lives to look forward to.

Very often at lavish family gatherings, at banquets of societies, much talk is devoted to home in the old country. People sing about the shtetl, although many of them didn't have enough to eat there and more than one lived in fear of pogroms. This doesn't mean, however, that they don't appreciate the good life that they enjoy in this land of freedom.